HELLO, LOVELY READERS.

Trigger warning.

Emotional, financial and physical abuse.

There's also cheating.

This is a FUCKING story. Not a LOVE story.

You can find me on Facebook under Shantel Davis. I apologize in advance for my craziness, if you do stop by.

Nicole Singleton is my editor and also accomplished writer Nikki- Michelle. Read her Bi-satisfied series and thank me later. SN: Don't read it in public.

PRELUDE

A man walks into a bar devising a plan to kill his wife. He jokingly asked the bartender if he had any idea how he could do it and get away with it.

The bartender poured him the two fingers of scotch he'd asked for then cocked his head with a thoughtful look on his face.

He said, "You ever seen that movie..."

SIMONE- DAY 0

"Try it on."

Shit! A sharp gasp skittered past my lips. My heart leaped to my throat. The sound of his voice had startled me so badly, I jumped and the necklace I'd been holding slid from my fingers to the carpeted floor. With eyes wide, I swung around to find my employer's husband casually leaned against the door frame in an expensive tailored black suit. With his hands clasped behind his back, he watched me. He was tall, at least six-foot-four and built unlike any accountant I'd ever seen. Thick corded muscle on an almost lean frame made him look like he played professional sports. His handsome face was devoid of emotion, but his cold steel-gray eyes were filled with a plethora of them. He stared at me with an intensity that scared me, throwing off my equilibrium. For a while, all I could do was stare back at him.

I had worked for the Alquist's for four months. This was the first time I'd seen Mr. Alquist up close. When I had been hired for the job, he'd been taking laps in the Olympic size pool in their back yard. I'd only gotten a glimpse of him when the wife was showing me around. I hadn't thought much of him then, but up-close, he was a sight to behold. His skin was so pale it looked supernatural. Short blond hair covered his head and strong jaw-line. His face was chiseled and rugged. He looked like a deity, the epitome of absolute power. Dangerous.

The devil has come to tempt you.

My stomach twisted.

Instinctually, I went to take a step back. However, like I

was being drawn to him, I stepped forward. I had to force my brain to still my feet and to speak.

"I wasn't going to steal it, Mr. Alquist," I said.

I tried to sound firm, but my voice betrayed me and cracked. I was terrified of being falsely accused. White folks would call the police on you in a heartbeat. His wife had already warned me she'd be watching me. "I know you people steal" she'd claimed, while wagging her boney finger in my face. I didn't know if she was referring to poor people or Black people and didn't care. I'd simply rolled my eyes when she turned her back. I was used to it. I'd been cleaning the homes of the privileged for nearly four years and had heard it all. They looked down on everyone who had less than them.

I learned not to take it personally. Her forced respect meant nothing to me. I needed their money. I had rent and law school to pay for. I had just gotten fired from another job for no reason. One day out of the blue, my old boss had called me into his office and told me he and his wife no longer required my services, then handed me a check, and told me to leave his property, no explanation. I didn't know what I was going to do, but luckily one of their kitchen staff felt bad for me and had directed me to the Alquist. They were paying twice the amount of what I had been earning and I did less because they didn't have any kids. I wasn't about to mess that up by snapping.

Mr. Alquist cocked his blond head to the side and smirked. "I didn't accuse you, Simone. And please," he said, his voice deep and raspy, "call me Seth."

I nodded, exhaling a pent-up breath. My heart rate slowed.

He said he wasn't accusing me, so that was my cue to leave. The vibe wafting off him was making me antsy.

I said, "So... I I'll get back to work." I took a step forward. Then another. He continued blocking the doorway and he didn't look like he'd be moving anytime soon. I stopped walking. "Will that be all?" I asked.

Instead of answering he dropped his eyes and gave me a slow perusal from my head to my toes, then smiled a slick smile, his lips curving. I swallowed. I could tell, he knew he was making me uncomfortable and he was enjoying it. Confidence. No, arrogance seeped through his pores.

I frowned then glared at him.

Finally, he moved. He walked with a confident stride further into the room. The path he took continued to block my path to freedom.

I spread my feet, bracing myself for whatever happened next as I carefully watched him.

With one hand, he smoothly unbuttoned his jacket, took it off, and slung it onto the ornate king size poster bed.

"I said try it on." He spoke softly, but his tone was insistent, demanding even.

"Fuck no," was on the tip of my tongue, but instead I forced a smile onto my lips before denying him.

"No. I'm good. I was just admiring it." The necklace was exquisite. I had never seen anything like it in real life, so when I saw it sitting out on the dresser, of course I looked. "I have to go back to work now. "

Frazzled and not thinking clearly, I turned my back on him. I bent to pick the necklace from the floor to return it back to where I'd gotten it. When I righted myself, he was behind me, right up on my ass.

His naturally masculine scent enveloped me. He smelled like fire and brimstone, like sin. My throat went dry. Another warning rang in my head. Intuitively I knew that moment was the beginning of trouble for me where he was concerned. I could feel it in my bones.

Shit! How did I let this happen? I wanted to kick my own ass for being nosey and putting myself in the position to be caught alone in the room with him. That was my number two rule. Never be alone with the husbands. Number one was never fuck them. Though rich white men usually married women who looked like barbie dolls, they would fuck women who looked like me. I had learned that to be true many, many times. If I had a dollar for every time I'd been propositioned in four years, I'd be rich.

They all wanted a whore, something new and exotic to fuck. My dark, almost midnight black- blue complexion, size eighteen body, curvy waist, big tits, light eyes and round ass made them want to indulge in me, if only for a short while.

I faced him, then backed away. I wanted out of his personal space and I needed him out of mine. He stopped me, by curling his thick fingers around my wrist. His grip firm, but not painful. He eclipsed me by height and weight which made it easier for him to pull me to him, even as I struggled.

He pulled me so close our breaths synchronized. He lifted his free hand then brushed his thumb across my cheek in a gentle stroke.

"So soft," he whispered.

Again, I tried to move only to have his grip tighten.

He held me there, looking at me expectantly, waiting. For what I didn't know. A thank you, maybe? For me to drop my drawls because he complimented me?

"I need to get back to work, sir." That sir tasted bitter coming out my mouth. My stomach roiled.

"Not yet. Give me the necklace." There was an edge to his tone. I'd be lying if I said it didn't turn me on.

He didn't wait for me to oblige. He dropped his hands from my wrist and face and removed the necklace from my hand himself.

He moved slow and deliberate as if he didn't want to frighten me as he brought the necklace up and placed it around my neck. My hands shook as my mind raced with thoughts of what would happen next.

The weight of the canary yellow diamond pendant came to rest heavily between my cleavage. The diamond gleamed and sparkled underneath the lights.

I looked down at it for a split second. "It's pretty," I said to appease him. I was losing my patience, with him and with the situation.

The urge to get his wife's necklace off my neck saddled me with unease. It felt wrong around my neck. It didn't belong to me.

I wanted it off. I wanted him out of my space. I wanted out of that house.

I raised my hands to unclasp the necklace. Seth gently knocked them away. "It's more than pretty," he said.

I frowned as I opened my mouth to say something, but before I could get any words out, he brought his finger to my lips. "Shhhhh," he whispered.

I scowled.

He grabbed my elbow. "Let me show you," he said as he led me over to the vanity.

I felt like a rag doll, my body separate from my mind. My mind was screaming for me to snatch away and run, but my body was allowing him to do with me as he pleased.

Seth stopped us in front of the vanity mirror. He moved so he stood behind me. He reached around and tipped my chin with one thick finger.

"See," he said. His eyes were fixated on the diamond that lay against my cleavage. "Look at it. I knew it would look beautiful against your dark skin."

My eyes drifted to our reflection in the mirror instead. The contrast between us was startling. We were opposites on all spectrums. Physically, mentally, financially.

We shouldn't have been sharing the same space. My heart raced. I needed to get as far away from him as soon as possible. But his left hand was splayed against my back, holding me there. I felt panicked, but the acceleration of my heart had nothing to do with fear, not exactly. I felt myself become angry. Angry that he wouldn't let me go. Angry that I didn't want him to.

"It's beautiful," I said again, giving him a pinched smile, hoping if I appeased him, he'd let me loose.

"*You* are, too," he said, putting an emphasis on the word you.

Our eyes met in the mirror. I couldn't put into words what was in his, but his gaze was unnerving. My skin exploded in Goosebumps. I decided right then that I was removing myself from the situation even if it got me fired. He must have sensed it. In that same moment, he pressed his weight into me. Wrapped an arm around me, hugged me from behind, fully trapped me against the vanity with his steel frame. Then with his free hand he reached up and brushed my hair away from my shoulder.

His full lips lingered only inches away from the pulse on my neck. His warm, sweet breath heated my cool skin. He inhaled long and hard, breathing me in. He had the look of a man savoring what he was about to consume on his face. And Oh My God! I damn near fainted.

My pussy pulsed and came to life and that scared me, caused my palms to sweat. I should not have been reacting that way to him violating my personal space. What was wrong with me? I was so wet; my panties became uncomfortable. My heart banged against my ribcage. I didn't know if it was fear or anticipation I felt.

"How do you always smell so fucking good?" The deep bass in his voice rumbled against my back as he spoke, "Every time I walk into a room you've been in, traces of your smell remain long after. It makes my dick so fucking hard."

He was hard then. Thick and long, his manhood was pressed into my ass. He made sure I could feel every inch of him. Every single hair on my body stood on end. What kind of married man said something like that to a woman who wasn't his wife, and why was my body on fire because of it?

I didn't know what to say in return. I had very little experience with men. I remained speechless as I watched him through the mirror.

What's wrong with you Simone? my mind yelled. *Stop just staring at him. Pull away and run!*

But I didn't pull away or run. I couldn't. I was frozen where I stood. Seth's fingers dug into my fleshy hip, kneading and massaging it. He watched me without blinking. His hands on me felt so good. I shivered.

He felt the tremble in my body and grinned, displaying all thirty-two of his pearly whites. He gave me a knowing look, one that said, "I know I can fuck you, right now if I want to."

He was right, but this was wrong. I should have stopped him. He kept touching me, manipulating my soft flesh. I let him.

Only when the sound of his wife's heels tapping up the stairs broke through the silence did he stop. His hands brushed the side of my breasts as he backed away. Even still, he lingered behind me, watching me in the mirror. His eyes chased mine, trying to convey a message with his look. I turned away from his gaze. I wanted no parts of what he was offering.

Tick, tick, tick, tick...

I was so keyed up, I could hear the sound of the clock ticking away. More than half a minute passed before I heard him silently leave the room through the door that led to his office. When he was gone, my heart finally began to slow. I stood there as if in a trance, looking like a fool, wondering what had just happened.

SIMONE DAY 1

The next day, I was on pins and needles and feeling groggy as hell as I cleaned an already spotless house. I hadn't slept all night. I'd just lain in bed, with my eyes closed and my brain working triple time—replaying what had happened.

I was ashamed of what I allowed him to do to me, ashamed of how turned on I'd become. I should have walked away from the situation, and I definitely shouldn't have been thinking about how good I knew it would have felt if I'd allowed him to fuck me then and there. I knew better. He was married, which meant he was off-limits.

However, I'd never been that wet and I'd never felt my body respond as intensely. For the rest of that day, I had walked around with my panties clinging uncomfortably to my pussy. How would I face him again? I thought about quitting, but I knew I couldn't. The money was too good for that. They paid me more than any of my previous employers.

"Just avoid him," I said out loud, as I pushed the vacuum back and forth.

However, something in his eyes told me he wouldn't make avoiding him possible.

I wondered what his deal was. Neither him nor his wife seemed to spend any time together. He most likely didn't even sleep with her. Though his belongings were in the master bedroom, the guest room and his office were slept in. I could guess why; his wife was a hateful shrew.

On some of the few occasions he had been home, I'd heard her yelling at him and berating him. When she started, I'd usually throw on my earbuds to drown them out. He could have deserved it for all I knew. But looking around their house said he probably didn't.

They lived in the lap of luxury. His wife didn't have a job and he always seemed to be away at work. He was fine and paid. The wife showed no signs of physical abuse. If I was his wife, I would have been happy. I wondered why she wasn't.

It doesn't matter, Simone. Do your job and go home, I chastised myself.

It wasn't my job to speculate. I knew I needed more vigorous work so I could take my mind off them, more specifically, him. I decided to scrub the kitchen floors, then I'd cook dinner and leave. Cooking was part of my responsibility when they didn't go out to eat. Luckily, I was naturally gifted in the kitchen.

I put away the vacuum and headed to the kitchen. Their house was huge: 10,000 square-feet, ten bedrooms and five baths. It took at least a full minute to walk from the foyer to the kitchen. I pushed open the kitchen door. The sight before me froze me in place. There was Seth's wife, draped over the black granite kitchen counter, being fucked from behind by her assistant. The *slap, slap, slap* of skin reverberated off the kitchen walls. She was screaming and moaning like she hadn't had any dick in a while, like the dick was too good to her. I wondered if her husband wouldn't, didn't or couldn't fuck her right. Morbid curiosity held me there, watching them for longer than I should have. Then I realized what I was doing. Horrified, I turned too fast in an effort to get away and collided with the frame of the door. Bang! My head smacked against it so hard the sound was louder than the wife's moans. It drew their attention immediately. I could hear ruffling and shuffling behind me.

"Fuck," I yelled. Dizzy, my head spun. *This can't be life*

"Why are you still here?" The bitch's shrill voice caused my ears to ring, as I turned to answer her.

Her assistant, Robert, was in the process of shoving his long, black dick back in his pants. Her thick white essence covered it. He smirked when he caught me watching him. I snatched my eyes away and focused on Mrs. Alquist, who didn't bother trying to hide what they'd been doing. Her robe remained open leaving her pale naked body exposed. She was shaped like the women on those nude magazines. Barely any hips, flat stomach, breast too big for her frame.

"Go," she barked over her shoulder to Robert before turning her attention back to me.

Robert pushed past me with a smirk on his face that read, "you can get it too". His eye lingered on my exposed cleavage like they always did when we had the misfortune of sharing space. He was a creep but had the whole tall, dark and handsome thing going for him. He was the typical pretty boy type, that expected all women to fall over themselves when he was around. At six-two with skin even darker than mine and an athletic build, with shoulder-length dreads, he would have been fuckable if he wasn't so smug. He'd cornered me twice in the short time I'd been working in the Alquist's home and offered to put a smile on my face. I'd declined.

Mrs. Alquist sneered as she looked at me. "What did you see?" she asked.

Her average looking face was all balled up. She reminded me of that chick from the movie Train Wreck. Her husband could have definitely done better, looks and attitude wise.

I shook my head. "Nothing. Your business is your own," I said without hesitation or inflection.

I knew how to play the game. I wasn't hired to inform her husband she was cheating. I cleaned toilets and vacuumed floors.

She stepped forward. Got right up in my face, wagged her finger. "You're damn right you saw nothing, and if you want to keep your job-- keep your fucking mouth shut," she threatened before shoving me to the side with her shoulder. I steadied myself against the frame of the door.

She walked out, leaving the stench of old sex and expensive perfume in her wake. It took everything in me not to reach back and snatch her by her stringy blond hair. Being a bitch was going to get her ass beat, especially if she put her hands on me again.

"Nasty bitch," I mumbled under my breath.

To keep myself from over thinking about other people's drama, I went about my business acting like nothing had happened. I was good at compartmentalizing

I spent the following thirty minutes on my hands and knees, cleaning the tiled kitchen floor. I was so ready to go home. The pungent smell of cleaner was burning my nostrils, my head hurt, and my back was sore from all the bending and scrubbing.

I was already annoyed and became even more so when Mr. Alquist's voice sounded off behind me, I jumped. "I need to see you in my office, Simone."

I turned my head in his direction to ask him why, but he was gone before the words formed on my lips. After seeing his wife getting fucked like a common slut, I thought the day couldn't get any more eventful. Worried, I stalled our meeting. I finished scrubbing the entire floor. Another thirty minutes passed with me agonizing over what he could possibly want with me. Had his wife told him to fire me to keep her secret? If that was the reason, she'd screwed up. I would definitely tell on her then. Should I quit and just walk out? Did he want to talk about what had happened the day before? All the questions made my head swim. In the end, I decided to go see what he wanted, hoping I still had a job.

***

"I called you in here because I have a question for you," he said.

Nervous, I scanned the large room as I waited for him to continue. His office screamed wealth and sophistication. On the right was a large cherry wood armoire. Inside I knew there were five suits in varying shades of Black or blue. All Armani. I'd just hung them the day before after they arrived from the cleaners. On the left of me was a large Black leather sofa, that like always, had a pillow and blanket on it. I quickly looked away before my mind could wander again as to why he slept there instead of with his wife. They landed on one of the framed pieces of paper that hung on the textured grey walls. There were at least ten.

I had never paid attention to all the degrees and certificates that lined his office walls. I just cleaned them and left. Seemed that Mr. Alquist wasn't just rich, he was very educated also. He was where I wanted to be. I could admire him for that.

When Mr. Alquist still hadn't spoken, I cut my eyes back to him. He was watching me again. He cleared his throat, and that's when I realized he was waiting for me to acknowledge him.

I nodded for him to continue. I just knew he was about to ask me about his wife and Robert.

"Have you ever wanted something so bad that just the thought of it starts keeping you up at night, you dream about it? Yearn for it. Can't think of anything else but that one thing." His gaze slowly raked down my neck and lingered on my breasts. "Ask me what it is I want, Simone."

My voice trembled along with my hands. "What is it you want, sir?" I asked then waited on bated breath for him to answer. Though I had a pretty good idea of what he wanted.

"You," he said, slow and easy as if he wanted me to feel his answer. He leaned forward in his chair and began to elaborate as if I had asked him to. "I want to lick your pussy, taste every inch of you. I want to know what it feels like to have your lips wrapped around my cock. I want to paint your beautiful skin with my cum. I want to know what it feels like to cum in you, have you cum on my dick. I want unrestricted use of your delectable body."

He was going for shock value. He wanted me discombobulated and it worked. Internally, I clutched my pearls. Outwardly, I inhaled so sharply I ended up choking. He watched me with a pleased smirk stretched across his handsome face while I fought for composure.

He didn't move a muscle to help me. He just leaned back in his chair, awaiting my response. I shouldn't have been surprised by his confession after what had happened the day before, but to have him put it out there so bold and direct was something else altogether.

When he realized he would get no response from me, he

pushed forward. "Do you need further explanation?" Seth asked.

Speechless, I shook my head. If he said anymore, I might embarrass myself by cumming. My clit was thumping, beating to a rhythm I had no control over. Wetness saturated my inner thighs.

"You want to have sex with me?"

He tilted his head as if studying me. "No. I want to fuck you. You're a grown-up, Simone. Say fuck. And I'm willing to pay you."

Did he say pay me?

Every part of my heated body went on pause as my brain replayed his words.

He had indeed said he was willing to pay me.

My head jerked back as if he'd physically struck me. I was appalled. My blood boiled in my veins. I clenched then clenched my fist. I wasn't for fucking sale. Rich people thought that they could buy whatever they wanted. I would never be bought. Who in fuck did he think he was?

It was my turn to tilt my head. "Excuse me?" I said. "Did you just say that you'd pay me as if I was a whore?"

Seth chuckled condescendingly. "You're offended that I offered to pay you? Why? Are you so used to men fucking you for free that you think-- to actually be paid for sex is beneath you?"

He shook his head. "Tsk, tsk, Simone. Would you rather I fuck you for free and all you get out of it is a wet, stretched pussy? Because that can be arranged as well." He licked his lips and leered at me.

I glared at him in return. He was a cocky asshole.

I couldn't respond right away because didn't know what to say. What he said made more sense than it should have. Made more sense than I wanted it to.

My brain throbbed; I lifted my hand and massaged my forehead.

"I also noticed that you were offended by the fact that I offered to pay you for sex and not by the fact that I asked you for sex to begin with." Seth's eyes twinkled. "That tells me a lot…"

He was right. The fact that he had asked me for sex hadn't been what initially offended me. I would have fucked him for free if he touched me again like he'd done the day before. His wife be damned. It had been the offer to pay me that set me off, but I had to admit, after listening to his rebuttal— I felt stupid for getting upset. Fair exchange is never robbery.

I took a deep breath to calm myself.

"How much?" I asked.

Seth grinned so handsomely it made my nipples pebble.

"Five thousand a month."

My mouth dropped open. "Really? Five grand?"

I couldn't believe it. Not only was he willing to pay, but he was willing to pay me for my pussy and he didn't even know if it was trash or not? It was too good to be true. I'd need my money upfront. I wanted to scream yes, but then his words sunk in and my brain caught up with me.

"A month. Not a onetime thing?" I asked.

What about his wife? But she was fucking Robert. Maybe they had some sort of arrangement, but then why would she threaten me?

Bitch, that's none of your business, just do it a truly fucked up part of me screamed.

He ran his hand over his five o'clock shadow. Bit into his plush bottom lip and eyed my breasts then my thighs. I fidgeted and tugged to pull down the khaki utility shorts his wife insisted I wear. With them and a white polo I looked more like I worked at a country club instead of cleaning houses.

He shook his head, "No I don't think once will be enough."

The glint in his eyes and the way he looked at me—all apex predator like—overwhelmed my senses. I swallowed hard.

"You're very blunt man, Mr. Alquist. But what about—"

"I told you before, call me Seth. Is your answer yes or no or are you confused about what I want and what I am willing to give you for what I want?"

"I'm not confused. I just want—"

"It's a simple yes or no question, Simone," he said, lips tight.

"Would you stop cutting me off?" I snapped, annoyed with his heavy handedness.

He leaned onto his desk, drawing closer to me, his leather chair groaned from the shift of weight. I felt like he was too close even though the large cherry oak desk separated us.

His nostrils flared. "Then say something I want to hear."

His tone was curt and abrupt, menacing. It put me on edge more so than I already was. I didn't know how to respond with words anymore. I understood he was trying to strong arm me and it had my nerves frazzled. I cut my eyes to the floor. Stared at the gorgeous brown and red Persian rug that lay there, while searching for the words to explain to him that I needed time to think so I could make the right decision. There was a lot that could go wrong.

He said he would pay me per month. Did I really want to be some man's paid fuck buddy for an entire month?

"I don't know how to respond to any of this, Mr. Alquist. I think I need time—"

"I told you call me Seth," he said, tone low. "And your next response should be yes, or you should be negotiating. I can see in your eyes you want to do it."

My brows rose. "Negotiating is an option?"

He chuckled. "No. So your answer is?"

"Why me?" I asked.

It was something I needed to know, then maybe all of this would make sense. Pushing out a deep, heavy sigh, Seth dropped his head. He was aggravated with me. I didn't give a fuck. I had questions.

"Does it really matter?" he asked.

"Yes. I want to know. This is mind-boggling to me."

"Well if I fucking must," I heard him mumble under his breath before leaning back into his chair.

"Because you're convenient. You're beautiful. You get my dick harder than it's ever been. There's a laundry list of reasons. None of which will change your answer."

He was right. I was still conflicted. The corded muscles in his arms bunched and flexed under his dress shirt as he pushed himself up from his chair. He made his way from around his desk, stopping in front of me. He half leaned half sat against the desk. He was casual today for a rich guy, top siders, khakis shorts and a polo. He matched me. I wondered how old he was.

He looked to be my age in his mid or late twenties. His wife didn't' look a day younger than forty. Again, I wondered how he ended up with her. But quickly dismissed the thought. It didn't really matter in the grand scheme of things. If I agreed, I'd be fucking him, not writing his memoir.

He stared long and hard at me before finally speaking. "I admire you, Simone. I worked my way through college and know how hard it gets, which is why I'm being so generous. I read your resume. You're in law school at the moment. The money I'm offering you will make your life easier, pay for schoolbooks, rent, transportation, correct?"

I nodded. It could.

"Well then...What's making you hesitate?" he asked but didn't give me time to answer. "Do you have a boyfriend?"

"No."

"Are you fucking anyone?"

"No."

He bit into his lip and leaned toward me. "Then what's the problem?" he asked, tapping his fingers on his huge thigh.

I couldn't name one problem other than he was my boss and he was married. However, law school was expensive...

The lawyer in me took over. I shifted in my seat.

"I want my five thousand up-front, the first day of every month of our arrangement. Once it's in my hand its mine to keep. No prorating or refunds."

He gave me a weird sneaky grin that made me reconsider but he agreed to my terms without hesitation.

I had morals, but I also needed the money. I was working my ass off trying to put myself through law school without any help. My uncle, my only living relative, owned a prestigious law firm, but all he would give me was speeches about bootstraps and un-paid internships-- that he made me beg for.

This was my chance at a come up. Even if our arrangement only lasted a month, with my regular salary and with what he would pay me, I'd end up with eight thousand dollars. If I added that to what I'd already saved, by the end of summer, I would have enough to be able to pay six months' rent and two semesters of school. Fucking a married man was wrong, but the end justified the means.

Fuck it!

"When do we start?" I asked, curious to know what he had in mind.

"We start now and here," In one fluid movement, he grabbed my arm and pulled me to him so fast it scared me. I yelped and tried to pull away. My struggle was useless, I still ended up flush against him. My soft breasts pressed against his hard chest.

My pulse raced. "Your wife's here and the door isn't locked. Not now," I hissed under my breath.

"I don't give a fuck. Let me worry about that, serve your purpose," he said against my ear.

He held my wrist in a vice grip. His lips were so close to mine we almost kissed. I turned away to avoid his lips.

"No kissing. That's too intimate," I said, trying to make sure that some boundaries stayed uncrossed.

No need for him to try to act like this was more than what it was, just sex. Seth laughed in my face, then tangled his free hands in my locs. He gripped a handful, then yanked my head back.

He took his kiss. Slammed his lips against mine. He nipped at my bottom lip, demanding I participate. When I gasped; his tongue snaked into my mouth in search of mine. He tasted like sweet liquor and mints. I tried to hold my composure. Tried not to enjoy it, but I got lost in the kiss. It left me reeling. His aggres-siveness turned me on in ways I didn't care to admit. The feelings that coursed through my veins like hot lava were new to me. Sure, I'd been turned on before, but not like this.

SHANTEL DAVIS

When he pulled away, his gray eyes were iced over. My breaths came out short and fast. "I make the rules, Simone. Do you understand?"

I nodded. He pulled my hair until I whimpered "Yes."

Then, and only then, did he let my hair go. With one hand, he continued to hold me like he was scared I'd run away. With his other hand, he reached between us and eased it down into my shorts.

He growled low in his throat. "You're so fucking wet..."

He found and teased my swollen clit with his thumb. Then slid two of his fingers between my slit, rubbing up and down. When he slid thick fingers deep inside of my pussy, my eyes rolled and eyelids fluttered, but just as suddenly, he slid them out like he had only been testing the tightness.

He went down to his knees, pulling my shorts and underwear down with him. He removed one side from my left leg, leaving the other side pooled around my right ankle.

"Look at this pretty pussy," he said from between my spread thighs.

He hissed then blew warm air on my exposed clit. I moaned. I was so in a daze my legs shook. I barely registered the movement as he guided me by the waist to the side of his desk and pushed me over it. My breast flattened against the surface. My nipples felt hypersensitive rubbing against the lace of my bra. My thighs were saturated with wetness.

"This is going to have to be quick, brace yourself," he warned in a low, raspy growl.

I registered the words and should have taken heed to his warning. He sunk into me in one stroke. He was big—bigger than I expected, so much so he stretched me beyond my limit. It had been over a year since I'd had sex. I felt every thick inch he had to offer. I screamed out. His hand covered my mouth keeping the sound from escaping. There was a knock at the door in the same instance. I knew it was his wife, she was the only one that was allowed to interrupt him when his door was closed.

"Shhhh," he aggressively whispered. "I'm not stopping."

I tucked my lips into my mouth and shut my eyes tight, hoping and praying she didn't hear us or come in. I was inwardly freaking out.

However, I could tell he was getting off on having her so close while he fucked me. His dick grew harder inside me.

"What is it?" he yelled at the same time he started moving his hips, pushing aggressively inside of me. His strokes were fast and deliberate hitting precisely the right spot over and over again. The softest moan escaped.

My pussy throbbed so hard it felt as if my heart had relocated there.

What would happen his if wife opened the door? I was a nervous wreck, but my clit was electrified. I didn't want him to stop. The element of getting caught made sex feel so much better. My entire body shook from the sensation of it all.

He kept fucking me as his wife talked through the door. "That lazy girl left early," she said referring to me. "I told you we shouldn't have hired a black bitch. I had to order dinner. It's here. Shall I have it sent up?" Her tone was bitter and impatient when she questioned him.

The pang of guilt I felt for fucking her husband melted away. She was a bitch.

Silence stretched between them. My heart sped up. My hands and knees shook.

I just knew she was about to open the door and demand him to come eat with her. Wide eyed, I looked back over my shoulder to urge him to answer her before she did.

He roughly shoved my head down onto the papers that littered his desk. He leaned into me; his breath was hot on the side of my face. "If you look at me with those fucking eyes of yours, I'm going to lose it and cum in your pussy. Is that what you want?" he asked, fingers digging into my waist.

Hell no! That was not what I wanted. It sounded more like what he wanted. My heart thudded. I frantically shook my head side to side. I hadn't been on birth control in a year. The last thing I needed was to get pregnant.

"Are you coming down to eat with me?" His wife asked.

She sounded hopeful. It was weird. Not even two hours earlier she was getting her back blown out by another man. Now she was practically begging Seth to eat with her? I didn't have too much time to dwell on the thought though. Her husband hit my spot just right and an explosion started in my pussy and spread through my body like molten lava. I had to bite down on a moan.

"I'll be down in three—" he paused, then cleared his throat — "or four minutes."

"Are you okay?" she asked from the other side of the door as if she was unsure.

"I'm fine. I'll be down." His voice was gruff, and heavy.

He didn't sound fine. If I was her, I would have wanted to know why. I would have opened the door. But she wasn't me and I wasn't her.

"Hurry down. I need to discuss these text messages I've been receiving."

"Yeah," he grunted, then I heard her heels clicking clacking away.

Seth strokes faltered, then he sped up. I knew the tell-tale signs of a man about to lose it.

"Don't cum in me," I whispered loud enough for him to hear.

He purposely ignored me. I was almost sure of it. He grunted deep in his throat before I felt him explode inside of me. I bit my lip to keep from loudly admonishing him, not sure if his wife was nearby. He pulled out of me as soon as his dick stopped jerking. Before I could say anything to him about what he'd done, he gripped my waist and lifted me onto the desk. The sharp edge of it dug into my thigh meat. I made a move to get up. He pressed into my belly keeping me there.

I hissed. "What are you doing?"

Involuntarily my eyes dropped to his dick. Heavy, thick and coated with my cream. It was still hard. I couldn't believe he'd managed to fit it inside me without causing any damage.

His fingers flew to his lips. "Shhhhh..."

He dropped to his knees. His calloused fingers found my

thick thighs, and he squeezed and spread them roughly. I bit my lip to hold back a moan as he planted kisses up my inner thigh. When he open-mouth kissed my pussy, my heart flatlined for a second.

"Seth..." His name forcefully escaped my mouth though I had been trying my hardest to hold it in.

He stopped licking me long enough to say, "That's right, say my name. Let me know how good I'm making you feel."

His cockiness annoyed me. I wanted to tell him to shut up but lost the words when he spread my lips with his tongue. I swallowed hard. He latched onto my clit. He sucked it until my legs shook, licking and swirling in between to make sure I lost my mind. He managed to slide his hand up my shirt and under my bra to palm my breasts. He teased my nipple. I lost it. My body went rigid and I floated through another orgasm.

When I was no longer twitching, he let go of my legs with no regard. I laid back onto the desk. His papers, and even his laptop, dug into my back. I didn't care. I closed my eyes. Panting, I tried to catch my breath. I had never cum so hard in my life.

It took a while, but as soon as the high from the orgasm wore off, reality hit. I hopped off the desk and started fixing my clothes, and he fixed his, smoothing out his wrinkled shirt and zipping himself back up. Both our chest heaved up and down for very different reasons. He'd done all the work. I was pissed. I'd have to buy Plan B.

"I told you not to cum in me," I snapped in a harsh whisper once I was done.

He walked back to his desk without looking at me and removed his cellphone from one of the drawers, slid it in his pocket then shrugged arrogantly. "It couldn't be helped."

I was offended by his blasé tone. "Couldn't be helped? You have control over your dick, so it could be helped."

Without acknowledging what I said, he walked towards the door. The smell of me and our sex clinging to him.

He had a full bathroom in his office and his room was right next door. "You're not even gonna attempt to wash up?"

"No," he said before he opened the door and walked out.

SETH DAY 2

Paula.

My wife.

My sentence.

My fucking warden.

My owner.

She literally owned me. Had brought me for the price of my mother's breast cancer treatments. The ones that the doctors swore would save her life but didn't. Momma died and I was stuck. When I met Paula, six years earlier, I had been twenty-four, working as an accounting clerk in her father's office. Paula was twenty years my senior, so I hadn't noticed her.

I was making my way through the building, fucking young pretty girls, with wet pussy and tight bodies. I was living the life I'd always imagined. My looks got me all the pussy I wanted, and my work ethic had me moving up in the company quickly. I wasn't looking for a wife. Then my mother got sick.

After missing more than a few days of work --the fact that my mother had cancer got out around the office. Paula found out and offered to help, if I married her. Her daddy thought she was too old to be single and she couldn't get anybody that wasn't decrepit as fuck to marry her. Even with the fake tits and botox, Paula was a plain woman. Being spoiled and entitled made her even less attractive.

The proposal had been out of nowhere, she had never even spoken to me, but I didn't dwell on the why. My mother had been the only person in the world I cared about. Just the thought of her dying skewered me, so I married Paula. My life had been miserable since.

Sometimes I found myself plotting her demise in my head. I imagined wrapping my hands around her neck and squeezing until she turned blue or pushing her down the stairs and hearing the satisfying sound of her neck snapping.

Maybe it would be different if she didn't use my mother's illness to trap me or if she's didn't constantly remind me that she was the reason I had anything. Maybe if she wasn't such a bitch I could have loved or even tolerated her.

I wondered how much longer I'd be able to keep up with the façade. I was slowly dying inside. I wanted a real life. Not to be trapped in the fucking gilded cage Paula had me in. The only good things that had come with being attached to her was the fact that learned to leash my anger. If I hadn't, she'd already be dead.

"You're not hungry?" she asked.

The object of my disdain interrupted my rumination. Her dull brown eyes bore into me from across the table. I dropped my head, avoiding them.

"I was just thinking about the threatening messages and letters you told me about," I lied. I didn't care. I didn't know what she expected me to do about them. "You definitely should call the police."

She shook her head. "No. That could bring unwanted scrutiny to the company. I'll figure it out." She sighed heavily like the weight of the world was on her scrawny shoulders.

"How? They could be from anybody, and you said they were vague," I said.

I picked up my glass and swallowed what was left of my gin then pushed my nearly full plate away and changed the subject. Her father had lots of enemies. If somebody was out to get her, I was on their side.

"And no, I'm not hungry. I already ate," I added.

I couldn't help the smirk that came to my face. I licked my lips and was still able to taste Simone on them.

Paula's brows rose. "I know that look. Who are you fucking now? She must be good at what she does if she has you looking all smug."

I raised my gaze from the table and scrutinized my wife carefully. Did she know I was fucking someone or was she fishing? I didn't need her finding out about Simone and firing her before she served her purpose. I searched her face for answers. Her eyes said she was fishing.

"Who are you fucking these days, dear wife?"

She shot me a pissed off look before taking the scotch she'd poured herself to the head and refilling her glass.

Instead of answering my question she asked another of her own. "Would she want you if you were still barely making ends meet, living in your double wide, sounding like the redneck hick that you are?" she asked. A satisfied grin across her face.

It stung a little. She was trying to put me back in the place she thought I belonged, beneath her. Paula liked to remind me that I would have been nothing without her. She said it so often that half of me had started to believe her. Even though I was college educated and worked my ass off for her father.

I knew I could thrive if I just took the risk. I'd learned a lot during my imprisonment in Paula's world. I could make money. I had business acumen. I just hadn't gotten to the juncture in time where I was willing to risk everything I had.

Still I thought about her question. The answer shouldn't have mattered, but it did. Ego aside. The way Simone had looked at me in that mirror made me think yes. She'd been begging me to bend her over that vanity and fuck her. And I wanted to so badly, but Paula had come home, and Simone had looked scared to death. I gave her time to wrap her mind around what we both knew would inevitably come to be.

I almost couldn't believe it had finally happened or how good she had felt, hot and tight around my dick. I was already anticipating the next time. For more than six months, even before she came to work for us, I had been fixated with Simone. Thoughts of her crowded my brain and she didn't even know I existed. I vividly recalled the first time I'd seen her. Paula and I had been invited to a dinner party thrown by Allister Sanford, COO of my father-in-law's company. She was working as a nanny and maid for the family.

I'd watched her the entire night, to the point of distraction. The contrast between her dark skin and her honey colored eyes was startling. The way her lush hips swayed as she walked had me feeling possessive and needy before I even knew her name. She was beautiful, with her loc'ed hair hanging down her back and a permeant pout on her full lips. I couldn't explain why but I felt that she would come to matter to me. I knew I had to have her.

Paula had later accused me of paying too much attention to Allister's wife. I'd laughed at how wrong she was. Blond and blue eyed had never been my type. But her one sided animosity towards prettier women often sent her on one of her jealous tirades.

I kept thinking about Simone for weeks after that party. Then Paula fired our maid, after accusing me of fucking her, and I had. I immediately thought of Simone. I asked Allister to do me a favor. I didn't feel bad about getting her fired because I made sure she was paid well when she came to work for us. Paula was happy to have new help. Although she didn't see Simone as competition, she'd been a bit prejudiced when it came to hiring her. I talked her down. Simone was hired soon after.

Since that first day, I'd been watching her. She sang when nobody was around. Danced when she thought nobody was looking. But I was looking. I watched hours of security feed of her. I knew I was losing it when I found myself jacking off to it. It was footage of her coming out of the basement shower. It was wrong, but I couldn't stop myself. Everything about her was so erotic. Her body was sinful, filled with lush, fleshy curves that looked so soft. I had no plans on fucking Simone at first, but I constantly wondered what it would feel like to be inside of her.

Just her scent in a room sometimes triggered me to imagine what her onyx skin would look like flushed and sweat-slicked as she rode me. I wished I had more time with her earlier. I would have stripped her naked and ran my tongue over each inch of her delectable body, caressed each and every contour on her curvy frame.

Wanting her so much was the reason I offered her the money. I didn't think approaching her any other way would work when I had a wife, even if I told her the truth about my marriage. Money made things less complicated. I decided to treat scratching my itch for her like any other business transition. Impersonal. No muss, no fuss. No feelings, no complications.

I had already crossed the line though. She was right. I should have kept my lips to myself. I usually wasn't intimate with the women I dealt with. I fucked them to satisfy my basic urges. They're pleasure never rarely mattered. But once I got a taste of Simone, I had to have another ... and fuck... It was sweeter than I had imagined it would be. It was a mistake; a mistake I compounded by fucking her raw. Her pussy fit me like a glove, and she was so hot and wet. Feeling her skin to skin was something I should have never done.

Now I knew whatever it was about her that kept my dick hard wasn't going to let me go after just one time with her. I was already addicted.

Paula cleared her throat.

I looked up from my thoughts and smiled darkly from across the table at her. "Yes. She is good, and I do think she would want me if I was poor again. If there were a she. I'm not currently fucking anyone." I taunted her.

She sneered at me. "You expect me to believe that?"

"I don't care what you believe. My dick is none of your concern. You made it so."

She had a thing for college boys even after she forced me to marry her. She cheated which resulted in her getting chlamydia. I had the test results to prove it. That changed the terms of our arrangement. Our marriage was now an open one. She didn't want her misdeeds being exposed to the world and more importantly to her daddy. I hadn't had to touch her sexually in two years. I had two years to go. I would never fuck her again. Touching her made my skin crawl.

The only reason I stayed was because She had an iron clad prenuptial that stipulated if I walked away, I'd lose everything, even what I earned. My salary was handled by an accountant and put into a joint account. I had an allowance so I couldn't save any substantial amount of money. She made sure I was beholden to her. And though I knew I would probably land on my feet if I left with nothing. I didn't want to lose all that I had already earned.

"Don't you miss me? Miss fucking me?" she asked.

Her expression was anxious; she was desperate for me to say yes. Her insecurity oozed from her perfuming the room. I swallowed back my cruel reply and it soured in my stomach. I hated dancing around the truth, but I couldn't come right out and say no. Even in the beginning. Every time I was inside of her I just felt obligated to be there. There had never even been the feeling of novelty that came with fucking new pussy where she was involved.

"Why all the sudden questions?" I asked.

Paula got up and sauntered over to me, her heels clicked clacked against the tiled floor. Swinging what little hips she had. She stopped when she was next to me. She lay her hands on my thigh and guided it to my crotch. My dick was as soft as Simone's ass. I smirked.

Her brows knitted. The disappointment showed on her face, her blue eyes darkened. Her hand turned into a claw on my thigh. She dug her long sharp nails into me it. We started a staring contest. She waited for me to flinch. I barely felt it, my pants took the brunt of her abuse. The fact that I didn't shove her away or do anything at all pissed her off. Over the years, I learned no reaction was the best reaction when dealing with Paula. She dug deeper. I smiled.

The kitchen door banged open. Her assistant walked in just as she was about to lash out further. I could see the anger from not getting what she wanted from me smoldering in her dull eyes. That was Paula's MO. Since she couldn't use sex to control me, she used money and an occasional violent outburst.

I moved my gaze to the assistant just in time to see his eyes shift from my thigh to Paula's face. He was fucking her. She had so little respect for me, fucking her assistant right under my nose.

Inwardly I chuckled because I was a fucking hypocrite. I'd just fucked Simone while she was right outside the door and had enjoyed it immensely and planned to do it again.

Robert was his name. I gave him a smile and nod. "Come and take her off my hands?" The snark and double meaning were obvious. Paula blanched, momentarily, but recovered quickly. He visibly cringed. I shrugged, then gave my wife a pointed look. Paula snatched her hand away and clucked her tongue.

"We will discuss why you smell like another woman's pussy and perfume later, she snapped before pivoting on her heels and heading toward the door." Let's go, Robert." Her shrill voice called to him, and like the errand boy he was, he ran after her.

It was easy to dismiss Paula from my mind. My thoughts immediately wandered to Simone. I saw fucking her becoming a liability, and liabilities were something I didn't need more of, not while I was trying to fix my life. That didn't stop me from wondering if she was still in the house. I got up to go in search for her. I already owed her five thousand. Might as well get my money's worth, right?

SIMONE DAY 19

I knelt before him naked. Roughly fisting the base of his cock with both hands elicited a moan from him. I flicked my tongue over his mushroomed head. The thick long vein that ran the entire length of his shaft pulsed; his balls grew tighter. He was close. Pre-cum collected at his tip. I stroked him faster. His breath caught and his body shuddered, but he didn't cum. We both knew this needed to be over sooner than later, but he seemed to want to luxuriate in the act of getting his dick sucked instead cum from it.

"Show me your tongue, Simone," he growled.

I didn't hesitate. I closed my eyes, threw my head back and stuck out my tongue, doing as he had instructed knowing the consequences of not. He craved sexual control.

He groaned. "Good girl." Then he used his dick like a paint brush to paint my tongue with his pre cum. The moan that left his throat vibrated his abs.

I couldn't help it. I rolled my eyes. Hurry up and cum, I screamed in my head.

"I want your lips wrapped around me, now," he said.

I wet my lips and obediently opened my mouth. I allowed him to guide himself in. I wrapped them around him in the same moment he was wrapping his hand in my hair. He guided my head, situating it so he could fuck my mouth. Roughly he stroked in and out, pushing deeper with each stroke until he was fucking my throat.

I gagged. He stroked deeper. I choked as his hands tightened in my hair.

"Fuck, baby," he growled low.

His thrust got faster, his dick went deeper in my throat, forcing me to breathe through my nose. He slid his rough hand over my nipple. My insides were boiling. His knees shook. The power I had over him was like an aphrodisiac. It made my pussy throb. I held strong against the urge to touch myself. That would prolong what was supposed to be a quickie.

"I'm going to cum soon, Simone..."

I knew that already; I could taste the salty beginnings of the end.

"Suck it out," he said as he fucked my mouth at a desperate pace, trying to find release.

I relaxed my throat and allowed him to push deeper, stretching my mouth. His dick throbbed then jerked. He called my name, filled my mouth with warm creaminess. I couldn't breathe, my head throbbed from the tight grip he had on my hair. My nipples were painfully hard.

"You made me cum, Simone. Shit...Be a good girl and swallow it."

I wanted to spit the taste of him from my mouth, but he paid me to swallow, so I swallowed. For at least half of a minute after he came, he continued pushing his dick in and out of my mouth even as he softened.

Immediately after, I felt his eyes trying to catch mine, but I kept them downcast. He recently started trying to make our encounters more intimate than they should be. I knew better, but he was an insistent asshole. His fingers gripped my chin as he lifted my head. My face was covered in cum and saliva, but he looked at me like I was the most beautiful woman he ever saw. He ran his thumb across my lips. I dropped my eyes and stared at his abs to distract myself from his intensity.

"Look at me, Simone," he said barely above a whisper, which surprised me. He was usually always loud and abrasive.

My gaze connected with his and I could tell he was in his feelings again, his eyes conveyed that.

"So beautiful," he said.

Again, I fought the urge to roll my eyes. Beauty had never gotten me anywhere. I was sucking my married bosses dick to pay for college. I tried not to cringe at the thought of my current predicament. Once in a while my conscience would try to get the best of me.

He caressed my cheek. "Where'd you'd get those eyes?" he asked.

"Your guess is as good as mine. They aren't like my mother's or grandmother's. I assume I got them from my father, but I didn't know who he was," I said before I caught myself and clamped my mouth shut.

The less we knew about each other the easier it would be to cut ties when our arrangement was over. His eyebrows rose. I pursed my lips and sat there on my knees waiting for his next instructions, but he just stared, taking in every naked inch of me that was visible. After eye fucking me, he lifted his eyes to search mine again; he was trying to read me. He was wasting his time. He would never see me, not the real me. I wouldn't allow it.

He said, "Can I take you to dinner tonight, Simone?"

I vigorously shook my head "No."

He frowned so deeply his eyebrows nearly met in the middle. "And why not?"

I dropped my head and sighed inwardly. Dinner was the prelude to fucking disaster. Why couldn't he just get his dick sucked and go on about his way.

"Because you're married. Dinner is too far. Stop trying to make this more than what it is. You pay me to fuck you. That's it."

He stared at me for a long while before saying, "Okay."

I frowned. "Okay?"

"Yes, okay."

Okay was such a simple word but he made it sound complicated. While I wanted to dig for a deeper answer, I left well enough alone.

A stretch of uncomfortable silence followed until the house alarm sounded. Saved by the proverbial bell. His wife was home. My heart speeding up was my only reaction. The first time he demanded I suck his cock and she'd come home; I damn near broke my neck trying to pull away from him. He'd let me go, but as punishment he'd fucked me right outside the master bedroom door where she was napping. I learned my lesson.

"Seth," she yelled.

A look of annoyance crossed his face, but he didn't tell me to get up. Sometimes I thought he was trying to get caught. It wasn't until we heard her heels click clacking up the stairs that he finally looked away.

"Go," he said, his tone authoritative.

Hurriedly, I scrambled to my feet up from my bruised knees and jogged into the bathroom in his office. I closed the door and locked it. I pressed my back against it and screamed my frustrations into my hand.

There was a light tap at the door. "Simone, I need you to stay late tonight."

I groaned inwardly. I knew what that meant, I'd end up on my knees again or bent over another piece of furniture or clinging to him against whatever wall he fucked me on. He was punishing me for not accepting his invite.

SIMONE DAY 31

"You like to dance?"

Startled I yelped and snatched the ear buds from my ears. My blood pounding in them replaced the sound of Black Puma's, 'Black Moon Rising'. I turned away from the sink where I'd been washing dishes from breakfast and found Seth leaning against the kitchen door frame much like he had been the time he'd caught me snooping through his wife's jewelry. I called that day 'day zero'.

He must have just come up from his home gym. Instead of his usual suit, he wore a pair of work out joggers and no shirt. Though I had seen him naked before I still gawked at his sweaty, glossy form. The scar across his stomach was his only imperfection. His body was sick. He was other worldly handsome, and he had money. I didn't understand why his wife was fucking Robert when she had him or why he was paying me to have sex with him. He could have anybody he wanted for free, but he was paying me? That shit just didn't make any sense at all.

My eyes got stuck on his carved abs and he noticed. He chuckled. I adverted my gaze to the tiled floor.

"You gotta stop creeping up behind me," I said.

"Or what, Simone?"

His voice was a dulcet, deep tone, the one he used whenever he was horny. I couldn't help it, my eyes traveled down to his dick. The tent in his pants confirmed that he was indeed turned on.

I groaned and rolled my eyes towards the heavens.

"What can I do for you, Mr. Alquist? You thirsty? Hungry? There are waffles leftover from breakfast."

I didn't bother hiding my aggravation. His wife was running me ragged in preparation for her snooty birthday party. I really didn't have time to suck his dick or spend thirty minutes bent over his desk.

"I just asked you a question," was his reply.

I narrowed my eyes at him in suspicion.

"What was the question?" I asked.

"Do you like dancing?"

"Why?"

"Because I want to know."

I thought about not answering. His now daily interrogations were irritating the fuck out of me. He didn't need to know anything personal about me. Neither did I need to know anything personal about him, but it was a simple enough question.

I shrugged. "Yes."

I turned back and started washing the dishes I needed to have done before his wife gave me something else to do.

"Thank you," he said. I wrinkled my nose.

"What are you thanking me for?" He was so weird.

"For indulging my curiosity, of course. What kind of dancing do you like most?"

I sighed inwardly. This man wasn't going to leave me alone. He was going to push and push until he got what he wanted. I figured the quicker I answered him, the faster he would be on his way. I hoped...

"All kinds, but as a kid, I thought I'd be a Black ballerina."

"And why didn't you become one? You move beautifully. "

"Thank you, but I knew I would not make it." I reached back and smacked my ass without thought. "You ever seen a ballerina with an ass as big as mine or one as black as me?" I asked.

He groaned. Right next to my ear. He had moved so fast and quiet; I hadn't even heard him get close to me.

I tried to take a sidestep, but he gripped my wrist and dragged me against him, trapping me, my face ended up in his chest. "What are you doing?"

He smelled intoxicating, like sandalwood and aggression. I

knew then I was about to get fucked on or against something in that kitchen. My body heated at the thought.

"I like your body and your skin tone. Everything about you is beautiful." His hand glided down my sides, past my waist, then moved further.

My heart started beating between my thighs.

"I want to take you dancing, but you won't let me do that will you?" he asked.

"No." It was a breathless rejection.

He rested steady eyes on my face. "Dance with me now then."

His hand stopped at my hips. He guided them as he moved his own. My body fell into sync with his. His dick was rock hard, pressing against my stomach as he swayed. I wasn't surprised he had rhythm. He fucked like he did.

"There's no music," I stuttered and tried to back out of his embrace.

He held tight. "That's not a problem. "

He leaned down, matching my height. He started singing.

"Take me to church.

I'll worship like a dog at the shrine of your lies...."

His voice was smooth and firm as he sang. It caused a fire to start in the pit of my stomach and spread.

Subconsciously I burned the moment into my brain, capturing it like a picture, so I could remember it forever. Knowing that nothing else as mind blowing as that would probably ever happen to me again. When there were no more lyrics to sing, he hummed the melody as we continued our sensual two -step.

My mind was fuzzy. I couldn't think straight. His body felt so good against mine. So good I got lost in the moment and forgot where we were.

"Seth," I whispered his name.

He pulled me against him harder and squeezed my hips. The butterflies in my stomach multiplied and took flight. His eyes burnt holes through me. I glanced up at him. We continued to move in sync, even as he leaned in, pressed his lips against mine.

He kissed me softly. So softly I swooned, like cheesy romance novel swooned. It only lasted a short while before I shoved him, separating us and walked away.

"Simone," he called my name angrily and forcefully.

I ignored him and kept walking until I made my way to the stainless-steel refrigerator. "Do you want juice or water Mr. Alquist" I asked loudly and just in time.

He frowned. "I don't want any fu—"

His wife was coming around the corner. I didn't know how he hadn't heard her heels as she made her way downstairs, but then he'd been distracted.

"Neither," he mumbled.

I watched out of my peripheral as her eyes zeroed in on him, then narrowed.

"You haven't left for work yet?" she asked, her words slurred.

She'd been drinking, and it wasn't even noon. I felt a twinge of pity for him. All she seemed to do was drink, berate him and fuck Robert. I'd caught them again, twice, since the first time.

Seth rolled his shoulders but said nothing as she walked over to the pantry and pulled it open. She rummaged for a second and came back with the nasty granola bars she ate in place of meals. Meals she desperately needed to eat. She weighed a hundred pounds maybe but was taller than my five-seven. She looked sickly.

She slammed the box on the island before addressing her husband again. "I guess asking you to do the job I gave you is too much."

Not once did she look in my direction or even acknowledge the fact that I was in the kitchen with them. I didn't exist to her. I pulled my head out of the refrigerator then closed it. I kept my eyes forward, my pace steady and tried not to glance at Seth as I made a beeline for the kitchen door. I pushed it open and quietly closed it behind me. I shoved my earbuds back in my ear to drown out their argument. She was so mean. If he was my husband—I stopped that line of thinking immediately. He wasn't my

41

husband and never would be. No need to speculate about what I would do.

Hours had passed, and I hadn't seen Seth after the kitchen incident. For once, I had been looking. I couldn't get my mind off what had happened. My body was so keyed up, I was looking forward to one of his sexual quickies. But he'd disappeared.

I stood at the kitchen sink. Watching all his wife's friends and colleagues entering and exiting the tent that was set up. The backyard had been set up to accommodate hundreds. She had catering staff and extra hands everywhere. I'd been resigned to the house to make sure everyone stayed outside and make sure none of the temporary staff stole anything as she had requested.

"Have you seen my husband?" Mrs. Alquist asked.

I jumped. What was it with these people startling me? I turned to face her. "No ma'am, I have not."

She looked good. Her face had been beat to perfection, and the sparkling blue evening gown matched her eyes. It was a striking contrast against her pale skin. The fact that she wasn't scowling helped too, but again she was drunk. She wobbled a bit as she glanced off into space for a second.

Then without another word she pivoted on her expensive heels and left out of the backdoor, mumbling under her breath about how ungrateful and useless Seth was.

I turned back to the window and watched her make her way over to Robert. I could have sworn I saw him roll his eyes when she motioned for him to follow her to the side of the house. I shook my head. What a frigging cluster fuck of a marriage.

SETH DAY 43

Her eyes widen and were filled with surprise when she cracked her door to find me standing there. Without saying a word, she closed it. The resounding click that followed it closing angered me. I was about to knock again when I heard the sounds of her chain being removed. The door swung open. The smell of her wafted out. She looked over my shoulder then out into the hallways behind me like she was expecting someone to be with me. My wife maybe?

When she found no one, she took a step back and arched an eyebrow at me in disbelief. "What are you doing here, Mr. Alquist?"

I obviously wanted in. She stood blocking the door.

"Is this an inconvenient time?" I asked.

I knew it was. It was her week off. I should not be at her apartment, at all. I was crossing boundaries, but the desire to see her after work had been stronger than decorum. She had been on my mind all day. That had been happening a lot lately, her renting all the available space in my head. The implications of that were serious and I should have been pulling away from her instead of finding my way to her doorstep.

She crossed her arms over her heavy breasts and looked me up and down. "Are you serious? Yes, it's inconvenient. You shouldn't be here."

The thin top she was wearing barely contained them. Her thick nipples pressed against the fabric. I wanted to touch her. She'd become my addiction. I looked over her shoulder into her apartment.

"May I come in?"

I meant to hand her the food then tell her I was coming in. A man didn't make suggestions or ask permission with women like Simone. They told them what they were going to do, but I was distracted.

While I waited for her to answer, my gaze trailed down her body and got stuck on her thick thighs. She had on the shortest, tightest pair of shorts I'd ever seen on any woman. They were pink polka dotted and hugged her pussy. The fact that I knew I'd be peeling them off her later had me licking my lips in anticipation.

She cleared her throat drawing my attention, I forced my eyes from her thighs and brought them to her face. She was biting her lip, like she could read my thoughts and they'd turned her on.

I smirked. "May I?"

She opened her mouth to say something which I was sure would be no. I wasn't about to be denied.

I cut her off. Gave her a crooked grin. "I brought dinner." I lifted the bag. "I went to Jakes Cantina. I wasn't sure what you would like so I bought almost everything on the menu."

She wouldn't go out to dinner with me, so I brought dinner to her. I knew her favorite were tacos from that establishment. I'd followed her twice after work and both times she'd gone there and ordered their tacos then sat outside and ate them while people watching.

I didn't know if chicken, beef or steak though. Not wanting to disappoint her by bringing the wrong ones I brought one order of each. I bought empanadas and burritos, too. She eyed the bag like she was considering letting me in just for the food, or maybe she was thinking about snatching the bag and leaving me in the cold. She continued blocking the door. I guess she needed more motivation than tacos. I stepped into her space, and I immediately felt static, the crackling in the air that always happened whenever the two of us got within a foot of each other. Electricity flowed through my veins.

I pulled her to me, could feel her heart racing a mile a minute against my chest. I gripped her neck, ran my thumb over the soft nape, leaned in and pressed my lips to hers. Involuntarily, or maybe voluntarily, she sucked my tongue into her mouth. She tasted like cheap wine and along with her natural essence. I waited for her to pull back and when she didn't, I deepened the kiss, while massaging the spot right above her ass that made her purr. While she was distracted, I guided her out of the doorway, maneuvered her so I stood beside her inside her apartment. She groaned when I pulled away. She wasn't as immune to me as she liked to pretend.

Intertwining our fingers, I walked her further into her own house, after kicking the door closed behind me. We were halfway through her small apartment before she realized what I was doing and snatched her hand from mine. I kept walking. She had books and a laptop open on the coffee table.

"What were you studying?" I asked.

"Torts. School starts back soon."

"What type of lawyer are you—"

She cut me off snapping hard and curt. "You can't just show up at my house, Mr. Alquist. This isn't part of the deal."

She could pretend all she wanted. I'd seen the lust in her eyes when I pulled away from our kiss. I could work with that. I toed off my shoes next to her red chaise. Her house smelled like her, like raw vanilla, a scent she wore often. It also looked like her, eclectic and dark. She'd decorated with red accents and black Ikea style furniture. Everything was cheap, but nicely kept. I took off my jacket and threw it across the back off her sofa.

"With as much money as I pay you, it should be."

She sucked her teeth. She mocked my voice. "I wanna fuck you, Simone, you said. Not, I want to show up at your house whenever I want. I earn the money you pay me by giving you exactly what you said you wanted from me: pussy."

I turned to face her once I made it into her small kitchen and set the food on the small table. She wouldn't get rid of me that easily. I had always been relentless and selfish. At that moment I wanted to be near her, and I would be relentless and selfish in my pursuit at being near her.

I asked, "You want me to leave?"

She squinted her eyes. "Yes." Simone's face was very expressive so I could tell she really meant it.

Ouch. I breathed in real slow. Her truth stung a little.

"When we finish dinner," I lied.

I had no plans of going anywhere. I removed my tie and tucked it away in my pants pocket, then loosened the top buttons on my shirt.

She eyed the bag again. Shifted her weight. "I hope you don't make this a habit," she said.

"I would never," I lied again without hesitation. I was already mentally planning my next visit. "I won't take up too much of your time. Just share a meal with me." I gave her my saddest eyes. "I had a long day."

My wife showing up in my boardroom tipsy and swinging her weight around in front of my colleagues had me wired with anger. Her father was sick and had left her in charge. The new power she wielded, and her paranoia was going to her head. She had also accused me of being the one sending her the threatening messages and letters she was getting. All the stress was causing her to drink more. More drinks equated to more outburst.

Simone twisted her lips before releasing a deep breath and giving in. "Fine. I'll get the plates, but you have to leave after dinner."

"I promise."

The skeptical look on her face said she didn't believe me, but she didn't make me leave.

Her kitchen smelled like she'd recently baked cookies and bleach. The sweet smells and simplicity gave off a warm feeling. More of my anxiety ebbed away. I took a seat at the small table and dragged my fingers through my hair to distract me from my need to touch her again. I watched her out of my peripheral as she opened and closed cabinets. The tension that had the muscles in my neck and back loosened. Her presence relaxed me. Things between us were getting deeper, faster than I expected them to be. At least on my part. She was fighting it.

"You want wine? A beer? Vodka or gin?" she asked casually after sitting a plate in front of me.

"Whatever you want to give me."

I meant it. Whatever she'd give me I'd take. Wine, beer, vodka or gin, a moment of her time, her body, her heart... I was in trouble and I realized it at that moment. Wanting to fuck her had morphed into wanting her, all of her. She paused to look at me. Our eyes met and an understanding passed between us. She was stuck with me.

She shook her head, then looked at me. "You're not leaving tonight, are you?" she asked.

"No," I answered.

"You're so obnoxious and pushy. I shouldn't have opened the door."

"I would have kept knocking if you didn't."

She cocked her head. "Really? So, you just showed up with the expectations of getting in? How did you know I wouldn't have company? Suppose my man was here?"

She sat a corona in front of me and took a seat across from me. I wasn't a jealous man and she wasn't mine, but I found myself seething at the thought of another man being in her space, touching her. I frowned, then rolled my tongue around in my mouth to keep my thoughts from spilling out. It didn't work

I bared my teeth. "Your man is none of my concern, but did you tell him I pay you to suck my dick?"

She paused as if considering the question, then threw her head back and laughed. It wasn't the response I expected.

"If I had a man, I wouldn't be sucking your dick."

My shoulders relaxed. "Why don't you have one?"

I removed the containers from the bags, opened each one and showed her the contents. She pointed to the tacos. I handed them to her. She filled her plate, taking one of each.

"Because of school and work and sucking your *married* dick." She stared me in the eyes and put emphasis on the word married.

I sighed. She insisted on reminding me I was married.

Every-fucking-encounter.

"I'm married in name only."

"In name only? What does that mean? Why marry her at all? She doesn't seem your type."

She took a bite and moaned like she did when I ate her pussy. I licked my lips in anticipation of what would happen later.

"She isn't, but she helped me when I was in need," I said.

Simone looked at me. "You sound bitter instead of grateful for that."

"Frankly, I'm both. My mother had breast cancer when I met Paula. She told me if I married her, she'd pay for the treatments." My chest tightened as I spoke.

"The way you're looking right now tells me those treatments didn't work?"

I shook my head. Unable to form the word no.

"I'm sorry to hear about your mother. I understand what it's like to lose one."

She zoned out and stared at the space behind my head. There was a moment of grim silence. Melancholy floated around the room, making it stifling. I watched her as she brought her hand up and rubbed over her heart like it was aching. I wanted to comfort her, but I hesitated to. Any time I took a step toward real intimacy with her she withdrew. She was fine sucking my dick, letting me fuck her, but god forbid I asked her a question or showed emotion. Her rejection reminded me that I did indeed have a heart and it hurt.

She spoke up before I could make up my mind what to do. "Let's leave the subject of dead parents alone."

I nodded, readily agreeing. "You should."

She snorted and changed the subject to something safer. "Yeah your wife seems the type to do something like that though. But that answers my question about y'all's relationship."

"What's my wife's type?" I asked.

"Nice white lady in public, ready to weaponize her tears at a moment's notice. Raging bitch behind closed door?"

I nodded. She had her pegged.

I asked. "So, you had questions about she and I?" I took it to mean that she'd been thinking about me, interesting

She nodded. "Yeah."

"Like what?"

"Why there was an absence of love in that house. "

I gave her a serious look. "What do you know about love, Simone?"

She took another bite of food, avoiding my eyes until she finished chewing. "I don't know a damn thing about it outside of familial love, honestly. I haven't even been in a serious relationship and after watching couples fall apart all the time. I'm almost sold on the idea that there is no real love outside of blood; only people using each other. But if there is a such thing, I do know it ain't being married in name only. One spouse fucking the maid and the other fucking the assistant."

She shrieked and her hand flew to her mouth when she realized what she'd said.

"So, you knew?"

She visibly cringed. "I sorta walked in on it." She dropped her head. "I'm sorry," she whispered

I laughed. "Simone, it's okay. I know"

She looked panicked. "Does that mean she knows about me?"

"No. We don't discuss our separate lives. We don't have a romantic relationship and you don't ever have to worry about her finding out about you."

She looked up and frowned. "So, you all are in some type of open relationship?"

"Yes. "

She shook her head. "Why don't yall just get a divorce and fuck other people without all the drama?" She leaned forward, pressing her elbows on either side of her plate.

"Money. She has all of it. I leave I have nothing." The words tasted bitter coming out of my mouth.

"So that's all you want out of life? Money."

"No. I want a wife and kids. I want somebody only for me."

"You're willing to put all that on hold for money?" Simone asked.

I nodded once. "Yes."

"Ah." She nodded then averted her eyes. "This some white people shit," she mumbled under her breath just loud enough for me to hear.

I grunted.

"So, what you're saying is she's you're sugar momma. I'm surprised. I took you for a rich white boy. I thought you had the money."

I smirked." I came from nothing, less than nothing. I grew up in a trailer park in Tampa with no daddy and no prospects."

She frowned at my revelation as if she didn't like the idea that she'd read me wrong.

"So, you're pretending to be the smug and pretentious ass-hole, or you learned to be?"

I rolled my tongue over my teeth again and raised an eye-brow. "You're trying to be insulting?"

She picked up her napkin and dabbed at the side of her mouth with it. Then she picked up her drink and took a sip. She eyed me from over the rim of the glass. "Sorta. You showed your married ass up at my house, uninvited, and treated me like a whore after imposing on me. You deserve a few digs."

"You are my whore," I bit back.

I knew instantly from the look in her eyes that my words had hit the mark. Her light eyes darkened to nearly brown. I didn't mean to lash out, but I was frustrated and tired of her throwing my fucked-up marriage in my face. Why couldn't she just take the money and enjoy me without all the negative en-ergy?

She lowered her pretty eyes to a glower. "You need to leave, now."

I didn't care that she was mad. She'd get over it. I picked my fork up and took another bite of my now cold food.

She got up, reached across the table and snatched the fork from my hand. I didn't react as she started clearing the table, slamming plates and cups.

"I said leave, Mr. Alquist," she ordered again.

"I'm not going anywhere." I leaned back into my chair. "You can't be mad at me for telling you the truth."

At my words, even more anger overtook her pretty features.

She sneered at me and jabbed her finger in my direction. "Fuck you, Seth. If I'm a whore, you're a fucking whore too. You're married to a bitch who belittles you, all so you can stay laced out in expensive suits and it's until death do you motherfucking part. I only have to put up with your arrogant ass for another few months, if that. Then poof," she blew into her palm "you're gone. and I forget you existed."

Ouch! She had a way with words. They wounded like deep punctures. Heat rose in my chest. Silence gripped both of us. Simone was the first to break it.

She slammed the plates back onto the table. "I'm going to bed. Lock my door on your way out, asshole. She stormed out of the kitchen mumbling angrily to herself, leaving me festering alone.

SIMONE DAY 44

I went to sleep dressed. I woke up naked and cumming; my back arched from the bed. My whole body spasmed. The thrum between my legs had tears forming in my eyes.

I didn't have to look to know it was Seth between my legs giving my clit long languid strokes. I could smell his masculine scent all around me. After weeks of being with him I had memorized what his mouth felt like. Knew exactly how his calloused hand felt gripping my thighs.

I wanted to protest, tell him to stop. Him calling me his whore was still fresh on my mind. I hated hearing the truth. I was his whore, by definition, but he didn't have to keep reminding me.

"Seth," I called his name and tried to tell him he needed to leave.

The words formed in my head but did not make it to my lips. When he suctioned my clit into his mouth, I was putty in his hands.

Fuck it. I was weak for him.

"Come on, baby. Give it all to me," I heard him say. "Let go."

I tightened my thighs around his head and floated through my next orgasm. I wanted to stay mad. I really did but my anger melted away. After, he kissed his way up my body, stopping at my breasts. I shivered. I hated that I was responding to his kisses, hated that I wanted more of them.

"Simone..." He breathed my name, then twirled his tongue over my right nipple, then pulled it between his teeth. It felt so good a tiny moan slipped from between my pursed lips. I fisted my hand in the sheets, refusing to touch him. He gave my left nipple the same treatment.

When he finally made his way to my lips, I was nearly delirious. He hovered over me and nipped at the bottom lip while his big hands massaged my meaty hips, digging his finger into my flesh. Those seemed to be his favorite spots on my body.

"I know you're not a whore, even when I treat you like one. I'm sorry. I promise to make it up to you. All of it." He then brushed my lips with his. My grip on the sheets loosened. "Paying you was supposed to make our situation less..." He trailed off in search of the word.

"Complicated," I finished his sentence for him.

"Yes, complicated."

"You could always end it now," I said.

He chuckled darkly. "I can't. I don't want to. I'm too selfish. I just want to—" He paused then pressed his forehead against mine. "Open your eyes, Simone."

I hadn't realized they were closed. I shook my head.

"Please."

I didn't want to see what I felt in the air. His feelings were stifling. I kept my eyes closed.

"Don't you feel it, what's developing between us?" he asked.

"No complications, Seth. Pay me, don't fall for me. Treat me like a whore if you must. I won't get mad about it again. No complications."

"That's what you want?"

I didn't readily answer. "Answer me," He demanded.

I had to swallow the lump in my throat before I could. "I don't know what I want, but this is the way it has to be," I said.

I couldn't let lust and money cloud my better judgement. I couldn't allow good sex and pretty words to make me catch feelings where there shouldn't have been any.

With his forehead still laying against mine, he said, "I know what I want, Simone. Ask me."

"No, Seth. Stop this! I don't want to hear it."

He laughed. "I would be more inclined to believe you if you opened your eyes and told me that."

I sighed; my eyes remained closed.

"I like you, Simone," he said, voice low and silky.

"You don't know me. We don't talk, we don't interact outside of sex. I know nothing about you. Under our current circumstance that's a good thing."

"I know your body responds to me."

It was my turn to laugh. "That means I like the way you fuck me. The end."

"So, that means we can fuck and fall in love or we could get to know each other and fall in love," he drawled.

I rolled my eyes at the first part before saying, "You may not like me after you get to know me."

"I will. I feel a connection to you. And you'll get to know me then you can like me too, as a man and you'll continue to like the way I fuck you."

I grunted. "I can't. "

"You can. Can't isn't an option now." He flicked his tongue across my lips. "What's your favorite food, baby?"

"Shrimp," I answered

"Mine is Simone. "

I snickered.

"Favorite color?" He slid the head of his dick over my clit and I hissed.

My legs involuntarily spread. "Re-red," I stuttered.

The head of his dick pressed against my opening. "Mine is whatever color your gorgeous skin is."

He traced his finger across my belly. A giggle slipped from between my lips as heat crept to my face. I wasn't the type to giggle, and I damn sure wasn't the type to blush but he had me doing both.

"You're so fucking corny," I said.

"And your pussy is wet, very very wet. You sure you don't like me, Simone?" he asked, his voice taunting me.

"I'm sure I like fucking you. Other than that, I'm just here to—how did you say it that first day? Serve my purpose and my purpose is fucking you.

He growled. "Don't use my words against me."

I smirked. He leaned in and kissed it away and continued kissing me long after it was gone. He kissed me so deep it made me whimper. Exploring my mouth with his tongue, slowly he built a fire in the pit of my stomach.

I loosened my grip on the sheets that had grown sticky with my sweat, brought my hands up, and ran my fingers through the silky strands of his hair. When he pulled away, I found myself reaching for him. He gripped my wrist holding them against my body. He trailed his lips down my neck, across my clavicle, then back up. My skin flushed. I tilted my head back to give him better access.

"We have a long time to get to know each other, Simone. I'm not going anywhere. And I already know so much about you." He ran his finger soothingly up the side of my cheek tracing my jawline.

"Like what?" I whispered breathlessly.

"You like it when I kiss right below your ear, right here..." He kissed the spot then moved down to the juncture of my neck. "You like it when I graze my teeth on your nipples." He did that also. "You like your clit stimulated before I fuck you."

He grinded his dick into my pussy, repeatedly brushing against my overly sensitive clit. I bit my tongue to refrain from begging him to fuck me, but my legs wrapped around his lean waist on their own volition.

"I've explored every inch of your body. Next will be your mind. Then your heart."

He slid his dick into me and started fucking me excruciatingly slow. Slow and deep. His hands and lips felt like they were everywhere at once. His touch, his kisses made me feel good all over. Fucking somebody else's husband wasn't supposed to feel that good. I gritted my teeth then squeezed my eyes tighter. I pretended he was mine and not hers, just to chase away the guilt.

Lacing our fingers, he placed them above our head. I arched into him. He rolled his hips. His thrust was precise, hitting their mark over and over. He had me cursing a and wondering what the fuck he was doing to me.

I came right out and asked him, "What the fuck are you doing to me?"

I needed answers.

"Ruining you. Making love to you."

He thrust deeper, sucked my pebbled nipple into his mouth. I could feel his stomach tensing. He was close to ecstasy, but I beat him too it. My body stiffened and my vision blurred as he wrenched yet another orgasm from me. To ruin meant to reduce. The word was fitting. I was exhausted mentally and physically. Not allowing me reprieve, he picked up speed, massaged my flesh, licked at my skin. I felt our connection grow. The energy between us shifted.

"This is dangerous, Seth," I whispered.

"How?"

"Nothing sinful is supposed to feel this good."

"I got you, baby. Just feel good and worry about the rest later."

He kissed my shoulder and sank deeper into me. He was confusing me by not fucking me like usual. I needed his usual treatment. Hard and rough, primal. I needed him to cum and go. I needed time alone to figure out what I was feeling without amplifying it with good dick. Seth and I should have never gotten to the point where we were. He should have never seen the inside of my house.

I gripped his ass, tightened my pussy walls around him, whispered his name sweetly. I knew what he liked too.

"Cum in me baby," I said breathlessly.

His grip on my hands tightened until painful. He sucked in a deep breath and groaned. my pussy fluttered, milking him. He growled my name as he came undone.

"You feel so good," I whispered in his ear.

Hoping he didn't hear it but needing to say it. His grip on me tightened even more. He'd heard me. When his breathing returned to normal, he pulled his dick out of me then situated us so we lay with my back to his chest. He pulled me closer.

"I know this situation isn't ideal, Simone, I have a wife and obligations, but trust me. I'm not wasting your time," he said vaguely.

I didn't ask him to elaborate.

He continued to tell lies married men told. "I'm getting a divorce. I want you not her. Just give me some time."

Everything he said sounded good, but it was unrealistic. Men didn't leave their rich wives for the maid. He kept talking. I knew if it came time to choose, he'd make the choice to return to his life of money and prestige.

I pulled the sheet up to my chin and tuned him out. I had always been good at ignoring what I didn't want to hear. I took that time work out my feelings in my head. I was in lust. Money and good dick had the ability to cloud a person's common sense. We lived two different lives.

He isn't meant for you, Simone, I thought.

"This is not love, romance, a relationship. This is business."

I repeated the words over in my head like a mantra. The litany drowned out the sweet words he whispered. All bullshit. I'd enjoy the pleasure and money and leave before I got in deeper. This was just business, nothing else. With all that being said...He didn't leave my house until two days later and I was sad when he finally left.

SETH DAY 47

After spending two days with Simone, I'd lost sight of reality and started to bask in the illusion that my life could be different despite my circumstances, but as soon as I stepped back into the domain I shared with my wife, those delusions slipped away. My reality? I was trapped, for another two years. Which seemed like forever now that Simone was in the picture.

I didn't want to lose her, but I knew she wasn't the type who was going to wait for me, even with money involved. If by some miracle she decided to stick around, I knew she would eventually grow to resent me. Those thoughts didn't keep me from wanting her though. Or make me consider letting her go. I wanted her more than I'd ever wanted anything in my life, and I was keeping her. I just had to find a way to do it so that it benefited both of us.

My mood soured steadily as I made my way through the house. I was making sure to be as quiet as I could. It was after eleven at night. I hoped Paula would be asleep. If I hadn't been concerned about wearing my welcome out with Simone, I would have stayed until she had to return the work. But I knew doing so would only push her further away.

She was scared and confused. I understood why, so I left before we had to have a real talk. It was desperately needed. I knew I just couldn't keep imposing myself on her or fucking acquiesce out of her or even paying her. I was going to have to prove to her that despite being married, it was all about her. On weighted feet I managed to make it all the way to my office without Paula rearing her ugly head. I closed the door before flicking on the lights and letting out a breath.

"So, you finally decided to come home."

I cursed under my breath. "Fuck…"

The muscles in my neck tensed at the sound of her voice. Distaste curled my lips as soon as my eyes landed on her. Paula sat behind my mahogany desk in a sheer white gown. Her brown hair was tied up and she was tapping her fingernails against the wooden surface. Drunk and sneering at me, her blue eyes were rimmed with red and a full wine glass was clutched in her free hand. The anger radiating off her made the room stifling. I knew I was about to have a long night. I hated her.

I infused all the calm I could into my tone before I spoke to her. "Paula, shouldn't you be slee—"

She cut me off with slurred words. "You've never been gone for more than a day."

She stood abruptly, causing her wine to slosh around in her glass then spill on to her hand. She rocked on her bare feet; her head lulled forward. I was almost sure she was about to tilt over, but she righted herself quickly. Focusing her attention back on me, she sized me up.

I took a deep breath and relaxed my shoulders. "I had a work trip."

An obvious lie. She had access to my schedule, but the truth wasn't an option.

"Liar," she spat. "You were with that slut. It's the blonde, isn't it? The receptionist. The one with the long legs and big fake tits."

I had never fucked the blonde receptionist or thought about it.

"She's probably the one that sent me those messages and broke into my car. Yeah, I know it's her. I wonder will she want you when I put both of you in the unemployment line." She chuckled. "Or better yet, I'll have her arrested for harassment and vandalism."

"I'm sure she had nothing to do with either, since I'm not fucking her."

"Liar," she screamed. She could barely stand as she made her way from behind the desk.

I thought about leaving, even took a step backwards. Sober Paula was a bitch. Drunk Paula was volatile. Add paranoia and her temper was like TNT. Soon as I turned, her glass came sailing towards my head. I ducked just in time to avoid it. It shattered against the door.

"I gave you everything," she cried.

Paula knew I never stuck around when she was throwing one of her fits which was why she bolted towards the door before I could open it. She slammed herself against it. Trapping me. She managed to wrap her arms around my neck. I easily stepped out of her weak embrace.

"I'm your wife and I deserve respect," she screamed in my face.

I gritted my teeth and rubbed the heel of my hand to my forehead to ease a tension headache that started to pound there. "Move, Paula."

I wanted to go back to Simone. Being there with her, falling asleep with her in my arms, her body pressed against mine felt too right.

"This is my house; I own it and you," she yelled at the top of her lungs. "You don't tell me what to do." She reached up and attempted to strike me.

I slapped her hand away. "Don't fucking touch me."

The momentum and her drunken state caused her to teeter then fall backwards on to her butt.

She glared at me from the floor, her hair all over her head. "Help me up, now!" Tears filled her eyes.

Anger, hot and burning filled me. "If this is your house, Paula, let me leave it. As a matter of fact, let me leave this marriage. Look at us, we're a mess. Why are you holding on? Find somebody who can help fix you."

She scoffed. "Why are you holding on? Don't answer that. I already know. My money. You can leave, but you leave with nothing." She sneered then chuckled. "You and the blonde bitch can live happily-ever-after in that piece of shit trailer your mother blew her brains out in. "

A deep, shuddering breath erupted from my chest at the mention of my mother. Her suicide was a memory I constantly fought to forget. Nobody but Paula and the authorities knew that she had committed suicide. After spending a year in remission-- finding out she had cancer again had been too much for her, she said in her suicide letter. She'd killed herself leaving me to find the body. When I found her, she had been dead for days, all skin and bones, pale as a ghost. I'd never forget them empty look in her eyes.

Paula knew she had hit her target. The smugness reflected in her eyes enraged me. I felt like I was about to explode. I saw myself go ballistic in my head. Tearing through the house. Throwing her down the stairs. My blood pulsed when I imagined hearing her neck snap as she hit the bottom. I hated her. At a loss for words, I turned away and looked around my office. I'd spent fifty thousand dollars alone on furniture, another twenty thousand on electronics. I had the best of everything. I looked down at my feet. I was wearing five hundred-dollar sneakers, hundred-dollar gym shorts. A fifty-dollar T-shirt. I was living the life I'd only dreamed of as a child when I'd go to bed hungry and couldn't sleep because of the pain in my empty stomach. Was I ready to give all of it up?

I clenched then unclenched my fists repeatedly to stave off the impulse to commit violence. When my anger settled, I turned and stared down at Paula who was too drunk to even push herself up from the floor, too drunk to even hold her head up. She was pathetic. I was pathetic, but I couldn't leave. Not with nothing. I'd already sacrificed years. Angry with myself even more than her, I shook my head and left the room, slamming the door behind me.

The next morning when I woke up after dreamless sleep, I found an envelope on the nightstand in the guest room.

What I said about your mother was in poor taste, was written in her assistant's handwriting.

I opened the envelope and found a visa credit card with

ten thousand written across it. I shook my head. Paula treated me like an abused housewife from a lifetime movie: hitting me, demeaning me, holding her money over my head and I allowed her. I really did feel pathetic. I pushed myself from bed, got up and grabbed the shoe box from the top of my closets shoe organizer and threw the card in the box with the others. There were at least two hundred others and at least thirty thousand cash. Enough to leave, but not enough to live the lifestyle I'd become accustomed to. I dreaded returning to poverty or anything close to it. I had already lost my mother the thought of losing anything else caused my heart to pound. I was stuck in limbo.

SIMONE DAY 57

My text notification went off. I paused Netflix to check my phone. I already knew who it was though. Since the day Seth had shown up at my house we'd been texting back and forth, or he'd call me, and we'd talk for hours about everything. I was surprised by how much we had in common with us being so different.

Boss Man: What are you doing?

Me: Watching Netflix, The Witcher.

Boss Man: Me too. "Toss a coin to your Witcher." We should watch it together. Can I come over?

I rolled my eyes. I had just left his house and he'd been over every night since the first night he knocked on my door. I needed to set boundaries. It was getting harder to keep perspective. I had to continuously remind myself that he was not my man and that he was only using me as an escape for sex because his wife was a bitch.

Me: No, I have to study.

Boss Man: You're lying. You said you were watching Witcher. Have you gotten far enough to roll your eyes at Yennifer and Geralt?

I threw my head back against the sofa and laughed because I had rolled my eyes at them.

Me: Gag Me with a fucking spoon. I'm so annoyed with their insta love. It messed up a perfectly good storyline.

Boss Man: I guessed that about you. Let's watch the last few episodes together. I'll bring ribs from the place you like.

My stomach grumbled at the thought of those ribs, but I had to say no.

Me: You should not know that information. We shouldn't

be spending these hours together, especially when we're not having sex. That's what I'm for. You get off and go.

Most nights he'd show up with dinner, we'd watch movies or talk, then we'd go to bed or he'd go home. Whores weren't supposed to become attached to their johns. I knew better, but my stupid ass was willingly participating in a situation I knew that would end with me getting my feelings hurt. I felt the coming disaster, but I still wanted to say yes.

Boss Man: Open the door, Simone.

Me: what are we doing here, Seth? Why even ask if you were just going to show up? Why are you trying to force more out of this arrangement?

Boss Man: I'm not trying to force anything on you Simone, I just like being around you.

Ha! The lies he told. Not trying to force anything? He kept showing up at my house night after night, buying me things. Giving me money. He was trying to make me a whole mistress. I chewed at my bottom lip. My eyes shifted towards the door.

I shook my head as if he could see me, realized what I was doing, then I texted back.

Me: No. Go home, Mr. Alquist.

He knocked. I untucked my legs, got up from the sofa made my way to the door and peeked out of the peephole. He was standing stock still with a perturbed look on his face, holding a few bags. I swear I could smell the barbeque sauce through the door. He shifted from one foot to the other and looked at the door like he could feel me there watching him. He raised the bag, confirming he knew I was.

Fuck! He knew how to get my greedy ass. I was hungry, but too lazy to cook. Then again, I could order my own ribs. Instead of five thousand this month, he'd deposited ten. He claimed it was to replace what he used when he came over. Which was nearly nothing. He always bought food and drinks with him. My bathroom was fully stocked with expensive toiletries he bought, and he had even bought me a king size bed to replace my full so we both fit comfortable in it. It was an excuse. He was trying to buy my silence on the subject of him visiting all the time. I knew that. But I dang sure didn't give the money back to him. I was earning every penny he gave me. Mentally. Physically. Emotionally.

I watched him press his forehead against the door. "I just need a little bit of your time, Simone. Time to get my head back in the game."

I knew what he was going through at home. His wife was constantly drunk and flipping on him. Plus, she was fucking Robert so often and openly— even Seth had managed to walk in on it. I felt bad for him and he sounded so…miserable. I hesitated before turning the knob. Something in the back of my head kept screaming, *don't do this, stop it now.*

He smiled when I came into view. I couldn't help but smile back.

His smile morphed into a smug smirk. "I knew you would open the door," he said.

He lightly shoved me out of the way. Closed the door and proceeded to take over my personal life again. He turned off the TV altogether. He dropped the bags he'd been holding on the coffee table. Hooked his phone up to my blue tooth speakers. Ari Lennox's smokey voice filled the room. He removed his suit jacket and tie then threw them across the sofa. He then slipped off his shoes.

"Getting comfortable?" I asked sarcastically.

He grunted and flopped down on my sofa. He intertwined his fingers behind his head and sank into the cushions. He knew I had a soft spot, filled with a few feelings for him and he had just played on them. I had to laugh.

"Next time you come by; I hope your smugness comforts you when you remain on the other side of the door."

He laughed and shrugged nonchalantly. "Yeah, right. I'm already under your skin, Simone. You opened the door this time. You'll open it next time."

I put a hand on my hip. "Cockiness got you thinking so, but I bet I can show you better than I can tell you."

He laughed again. I was a joke to him

"Okay, sure. Come eat. You're going to need the energy." He bit into his lip. "Since you're so worried about me being here without us having sex, I plan on fucking you all night."

Shamefully, my pussy twitched in anticipation but at the same time I was thinking I had to put real restrictions on whatever it was developing between the two of us before it got out of hand. But the reality of the situation was the dynamics had already shifted.

SETH DAY 64

"You slut. Stay the fuck away from my husband."

I heard Paula before I saw her. I dropped my briefcase in the elevator and ran toward her voice. I turned the corner that led to the reception area to find her being held back by the fiancé of the blonde receptionist. She was wearing the same blue, floor length mermaid dress she'd worn to a fundraiser the night before. But it was now wrinkled and her once perfectly coifed hair was askew, and her face was flushed like it always looked when she was hungover. She must have spent the night drinking, but I wouldn't know. The moment the obligation I made to her was over I'd gone to Simone's.

"Mrs. Alquist. I have never had sex with your husband."

The blonde, whose name I couldn't recall, had fat tears running down her rose stained cheeks. I knew her fiancé Carson though, he was head of the mailroom and he looked pissed.

Paula pushed Carson and attempted to lunge at my receptionist, but he held her tight. "You are a lying bitch. Pack your shit. You're fired."

Nearly every employee, except the executives, were watching the spectacle Paula was putting on. It was obvious she was drinking again. It wasn't even nine o'clock in the morning. I knew her outburst would make it to the higherups within minutes.

"Everybody get back to work," I roared.

Everybody scattered before I grabbed ahold of my wife, snatching her from Carson. He immediately went to comfort his woman. I purposely applied too much pressure to Paula's abdomen when I wrapped my arm around her. Anymore and I could have cracked her ribs.

"Let me fucking go," Paula slurred and kicked out.

"I will email your daddy the pics of you and your assistant if you don't calm the fuck down," I whispered in her ear.

Paula settled in my arms. I turned and gave my attention to the blond; she was visibly shaking. I lowered my tone when I spoke to put her at ease. The company did not need a lawsuit.

"You're not fired. You and your fiancé take the next two weeks off, paid."

Not waiting for her to respond, I carried Paula to my office, ignoring the eyes burning holes in me. I dropped her like a sack of potatoes as soon as my office door was closed.

"Ouch," she cried out.

Clenching my jaw and balling up my fist, I shook my head and looked down at her. "Why would you come here and embarrass me?"

She laughed and pointed a manicured finger at me. "You're an embarrassment already, trailer trash with the dead momma Wah, wah. Look at your face at even the mention of the dead bitch who didn't love you enough to stay alive, you're pathetic and weak."

"Enough," I shouted, truly fed up.

Before I could stop myself, I'd reached for her. By her hair I'd dragged her from the floor and lifted her off the ground. Just as quickly as she'd let vitriol about my dead mother slip out of her mouth, my hands had curled around her throat, cutting off her air supply, silencing her. I guided her until her back hit the office wall with a thud that reverberated off the walls. She was forced to stand on her tip toes.

My mind raced, my thoughts bouncing around in my head. I thought this was it; the day I freed myself from one prison just to be locked in the next. At the moment not even going to prison made me reconsider what I was doing. My grip tightened. I felt like my old self again. She gasped like someone drowning.

The sound gave me satisfaction, enough to ease my grip. "Six years you've been disrespecting me, belittling and hitting me without recourse or retaliation, that ends today. "

Eyes wide, her chest rose then crashed. Her thin arms flailed out of control in an attempt to save herself, but I held her out of reach. Applied a bit more pressure. She gurgled. Her face turned a shocking color of blue as her hands fell to her side.

My head swam from the rush of adrenaline that shot through me. It would be so easy to shut her up permanently if I just squeezed a little longer and harder. Drool oozed from between her lips. My blood boiled. I kept squeezing. When her eyes looked ready to pop from her head, I finally let her go. Ragged gasps escaped her throat, her body sagged. I kept her upright by fisting her hair.

I pressed her face into the wall and leaned in real close." I will be your fucking ruin. I don't even care about the money anymore." I felt bitterness so deep down inside of me my bones ached from it. "My only goal from this day forward is to make you as miserable as you've made me."

I let her go. She sagged to the ground. A strangled cry pierced the air as I walked out of the office slamming the door behind me. I didn't even know where I was going. I just needed to get the hell away from her.

SIMONE DAY 67

Seth was making a liar out of me. I told him I wouldn't open the door for him when he showed up unannounced, but I did. We had been spending even more time together. We were no longer just business; we were having a full-blown affair. The fact burrowed under my skin. It irritated me, made me squirm and itch. I didn't want to be anybody's mistress. I knew it would end with heartache, but the way he made me feel made it seem worthwhile.

He pressed a kiss into the back of my hair. Breaking into my thoughts, he asked, "What are we having for dinner?"

We sat together on my sofa; butt-ass naked, fresh from the shower. He had me wrapped in his arms as we watched Creed II. I side-eyed him then shrugged.

He said, "I could cook, or we could go out, pick up something and bring it back home or we can stay out. Eat, go dancing, come back home. Make love."

We'd gone from fucking to making love.

We.

Home.

Make love.

Those words echoed in my head, bouncing off my skull. There we were, acting like a full-blown couple. He'd shown up angry and said he needed to do something to take his mind off his problem—not problems—problem. I knew he was referring to his wife. He took over my life for the next two days. We went to Busch Gardens and the farmers market. We walked hand and hand through the grocery store like he wasn't married. I was petrified someone would see us. He didn't seem to care.

He bought me things, gave me his undivided attention. Did things that men did when they wanted women to fall in love with them. Then that very morning at breakfast, after he cooked for me, he'd fixed my plate then his own and sat across the table from me. Before I could even taste the food, he looked at me with a serious look in his eyes and asked me did I believe in love at first sight. I didn't.

I tried not to read too much into the question, but I did. Read the fuck out it and came to a conclusion that his question had been in reference to me. I was too afraid to ask him if I was right, so I'd changed the subject and he allowed me. Even though, I didn't want it to, the thought of him loving me had buried itself in my chest, right next to my heart and wouldn't leave. It made me feel things I didn't want to feel. I wasn't making much effort to block out. Fuck him for making me feel them.

I really wanted to vent my frustrations to someone. The first person I thought about was Vincent. We had been friends during high school, that turned into friends with benefits in college. But I hadn't talked to him in nearly a year, and I couldn't call him with Seth there.

I glared toward the door front door. It was so close, if I just said the word, he'd be gone within minutes. I opened then closed my mouth. I wasn't brave enough to come right out and say it, so I brought up his wife. I did that whenever things were getting too complex between us. It was a reminder for both of us. He hated it. His eyes would go dark every time and he'd get all pissy.

"Should I make reservations?" he asked.

"Don't you have to go home soon?"

His body stiffened; he unwrapped his arms from around me. He turned me so I faced him. "You don't want me here, Simone?"

He stared hard. His face was unreadable, but the muscle in his shoulders taut.

Pressure built inside my chest. "It's not that I—"

He shook his head roughly, cutting me off. "It's a yes or no question, Simone."

I felt the tension and heard the intensity in his tone, so I knew to only say yes or no.

"Yes, I want you here."

I did want him there. I couldn't even lie to him though I needed to. He dragged his hand down his face like I had really aggravated him. He shook his head then closed his eyes and inhaled. When he opened them again, I watched his whole demeanor change. I saw the rough edges he had smoothed over with money and power become visible.

The corner of his lip twitched. "Shit, then chill the fuck out."

My eyebrows flew up, I was surprised by the bass in his voice and his relaxed vernacular. Did the white boy just try to check me?

Laughing I shoved him in his chest. "Okay, I'll ch—" I gasped when he snatched me by my arms and pulled me on top of him.

He did it so fast it scared me speechless. He watched me with a hooded expression as he studied my face as his thumb dug into the small of my back. He had something to say. I raised an eyebrow and waited.

It seemed like an eternity passed before he spoke, before he did, he licked his lips. Anger flickered in his eyes. "Are you trying to piss me off, again. Did I say something to make you angry?"

I shook my head. "No."

He frowned. "Then you're trying to push me away?"

Before I could answer, he slid his fingers up my thigh, grazing my moist clit. On their own volition, my legs spread allowing him greater access. A predatory smile came to his lips. One I was too familiar with, it meant trouble for me.

"Keep it up, Simone. The more you push and fight the more I want to possess you."

"All these declarations and you're marr—"

"Hush, Simone. You talk too much."

He leaned in and sucked my right nipple into his hot mouth while his fingers circled my clit. The rest of my words died in my throat; my breath caught in my chest. His hot mouth felt so good on me.

He went to pull away, I ran my fingers through his blond hair, gripped it and held his head to my breast forcing him to continue. He chuckled.

I moaned, threw my head back and allowed myself to enjoy his slippery fingers doing magic tricks on my clit. I was so close to cumming but suddenly he snatched his head from my grip and pulled away.

"Why did you stop?" I asked, sounding way more pitiful than I should have. The dull ache thrumming between my thighs made me not care at the moment. I was so close.

"You're mine, Simone," he stated matter-of-factly.

His voice was made sexier by a low growl. He flipped me so I was on my back. Did it so fast it scared me. My brain went hazy, leaving my body in a state of confusion. He had me ready to beg.

I grinded into him as he laid in between my spread legs and fixed his eyes on mine. He pressed a hand into soft belly to still me. I pouted but stayed still. He looked like he had something he wanted to say but was trying to choose the next words he said to me carefully.

"You make me feel grounded again. I haven't felt connected to anyone since my mother died, but you changed that. I also feel less fucking angry and trapped. I'm not—"

I interrupted him. "I don't really think this is something we should be discussing." You're about to go deeper than we need to go. Let's just enjoy—"

He frowned hard, then cut me off and continued where he left off like I hadn't tried to give him an out. "I'm not ready to let you go, might not ever be," he whispered against my pulse before his hand shot up. He ran his fingertips across my lips then further down. His hand came to rest on my throat, he gripped my neck applying pressure. Heat shot through me and I whimpered.

A devilish grin washed away his brooding expression. "I told you before you've gotten under my skin. Tell me I've done the same. I need to hear it regardless of my circumstances. Say you're mine, Simone," he demanded, his voice raspy.

Something in me wouldn't let me give in and say those

words. I couldn't allow my mind to wrap around the possibilities.

"For as long as you're paying me," I replied snidely.

He chuckled, but not humorously. "Why are you fighting this? I can feel it. You know you're mine. Give in, Simone."

He let go of his hold on my neck, leaned in and slid his tongue into my mouth while grinding his dick into my middle. His fingers feathered over my hips, my stomach. A hissing sound slipped from between our sealed lips. Just as it was getting really good, he pulled away. Leaving me breathless and yearning.

He said, "Whatever this is gotta work. I'm addicted. You're like a shot of heroine."

His pushed his dick against my opening, teasing me, but not for too long. My mouth flew open in a silent scream when suddenly he slammed into me. I dug my nails into his shoulders.

"Fuck, baby... You got the hottest pussy I've ever been in."

Grabbing my legs, he threw both over his shoulders, gripped my ass and spread it, slipping deeper.

I inhaled sharply. "Oh. MY God." He felt so big. "Seth," I whispered. "Please." I needed him to move.

He didn't start pounding like I expected him to. No, he rolled his hips. Thrusting in and out, in and out.

"Look at me, Simone."

I struggled with his command. I didn't want to. There is something inherently intimate about staring into someone's eyes. Too much intimacy to be engaging in with a married man. But I did anyways.

"You close your eyes this time, trying to run from me again and there will be consequences," he warned.

There was irritation and anger in his threat. And even though I knew eye contact during sex could be dangerous, I kept my eyes open. He was too skilled with the things he did to my body. His dick felt too good inside of me to deny him.

Holding my gaze, he asked, "Do you feel that, baby?"

I nodded. I felt it. Whatever it was frightened me. I couldn't even lie to myself anymore. I was starting to feel emotionally attached to him, but I wouldn't tell him that.

The moment my eyes started to lull shut he leaned down and nipped at my chin. "He snarled while saying, "Don't close your eyes."

He grabbed my jaw, applied pressure to focus my attention, making sure I kept our eyes connected. His were so intense.

"You're what I want, Simone. I won't allow anything to keep me away from what I want, not even you."

He then gave me slow strokes to make his point then quick strokes to make sure I understood. My insides were liquid.

"I've wanted this since the moment I saw you," he said.

My body felt so loose.

"I want you, Simone."

The speed of his thrust picked up. I felt like I was going into sensory overload. I felt him everywhere.

"Fuck…" we moaned in sync.

He hissed. "Wanted to feel you like this since I first saw you."

My hips undulated. I demanded more as my orgasm was steady building, rising. I clawed at his back, heard my pulse in my ears, hissed through tight set teeth as he fucked me like he loved me. I couldn't breathe.

"I need you, Simone."

My orgasm built like water currents, rising threatening to drown me. He was doing everything right.

"Steady now, baby." He dropped my legs and slowed down and just rocked into me, leaned in and took my pebbled nipple in his mouth.

I really couldn't fucking breathe.

"You're shaking," he said.

I was drowning.

He smiled, deviously. "Are you mine, Simone?"

I nodded.

"Say the words," he demanded.

I did without hesitation. "I'm yours."

There was no need to lie. I felt like his. All that had been left to do was say it. There was no turning back. Wed crossed even further over the line. That night Seth fucked me until he made his point very clear. Luckily for me I was naturally cynical about everything and everyone. I only half believed him.

SIMONE DAY 72

"I'm not doing this anymore, Paula. Consider this my resignation."

I walked into the house just in time to hear Robert yell those words through the kitchen door. Mrs. Alquist cried and begged him not to leave her.

Her voice cracked as she pleaded with him. "Please. Robert. I can't divorce right now, not with my father on his deathbed."

I cringed and backed away from the door so there was no way of hearing the rest of the conversation. Seemed like my employer's week was going from bad to worse. Seth had told me about her outburst at his office. He was spending more and more time away from home and his absence seemed to cause her to drink more. The day after the office incident happened, I had come to work to find two empty scotch bottles and one wine bottle in the trash and she'd slept all day.

Now she was losing her lover and her father was dying. I actually felt sorry for her. Rich White Lady, RWL, syndrome probably hadn't equipped her with the ability to handle everything that was happening to her.

I heard, "Bitch" being yelled followed by the sound of something crashing and her calling Robert everything but a child of God. I felt less sorry for her by the second. I backtracked and walked right back out of the door. I knew it would only be a matter of time before her rage turned on me. Seth had showed me his scars and I could never put up with it, so I was quitting. I would tell Seth and let him deal with it.

School was starting school anyway. Seth had given me nearly twenty-five grand. I was set for the semester. I closed the door behind me, made my way back to my car and drove back home. The entire time I wondered what would happen between Seth and I since I no longer worked for him. When I called to tell him I'd quit, he didn't even ask why. He just said he would handle it.

"I'll be over later," He said.

He never made it over.

SIMONE DAY 80

I hadn't seen or heard from Seth in almost a week when I received his fuck off text. It was nothing short of heartache.

Seth- Her father died. They'll be more scrutiny on me now. I need at least six months to get things in order then we'll start over from there. Your payments will continue to be deposited until then. Take care of yourself, Simone.

Take care of myself? Wow! My head pounded. Tears pricked my eyes, but I refused to let them fall. I knew it was coming. No married man leaves his rich wife for the maid. I knew it. That's why I only half believed what he'd said. It still hurt, like blunt force trauma the pain made me dizzy. My stomach tightened, and it didn't help that my mind kept replaying our time together on a loop. Each kiss and touch had been better than the one before. Each promise more convincing. He really had my nose wide open, half believing we might actually be more than we were, what we started as.

The levees broke. Tears flowed down my cheek. Crying made me angry. In that moment, the anger protected me from the pain. I shouldered away the tears. Fuck him. He wasn't worth crying over. I had already gotten everything I needed from him in the form of money and a hard lesson I wouldn't have to learn later.

I picked up and scrolled through my phone until I got to his contact. My heart beat a quick staccato as my finger hovered over the words block. I hesitated for a short while trying to figure out if I was being too quick to block him. Afterall, he was still paying me. Fuck him. I blocked his number and thanked God I hadn't let myself fall too deep in love with someone else's husband. Seth was right where he belonged, with his wife.

SETH

Eerie silence dwelled at the gravesite. Beads of sweat dried against my skin. Uncomfortable, the harsh Florida heat had me tugging at the neckline of my suit. The funeral was a gathering of all black clothes, fake grief and fake tears. Paula's father would be fake missed like most powerful men, because he'd been ruthless in building his empire, but also effective. He was leaving his only child nearly a billion dollars and an opportunity to make a billion more, which she was putting me in charge of. Paula seemed to be the only one truly grieving his death. She'd been crying for days. Once that first tear broke free, the rest followed in an unbroken stream.

I stood at her side feeling heavy and grief stricken, remembering the day I'd watched my mother's casket being lowered into the ground. Paula's father's coffin was pulled from the hearse by six strong men who didn't even know him. All had been hired and were all wearing expensive black suits that Paula had paid for when no one volunteered. I rubbed my neck and took deep breaths.

Everyone else's heads were down. Maybe it was them showing respect or maybe they were too afraid to look up and show they didn't really care that Gregory was dead. They were all there only because etiquette dictated it.

Paula wobbled at my side, using my body to keep herself propped up. I wrapped an arm around her waist. Even with my ill feelings about her, I felt bad for her. It wasn't easy losing a parent. I entwined our fingers. Her hand trembled in mine.

I could feel her eyes burning a hole in the side of my face. Reluctantly, I pulled my attention from the gaping hole in the ground. I looked down at her.

She looked up at me with puffy red eyes and said, "This is so hard. Thank you for giving me another chance."

Annoyance crept up my spine. I felt guilt, my stomach roiled. The day after her father died, Paula asked me to forgive her and work on our marriage. I was supposed to be giving my marriage a try. I agreed, knowing that it would make the two years I had left more bearable, at least I hoped it would. Thoughts of Simone and the promises I'd made kept haunting me. I was continuously thinking about what I was losing if I stayed. The money and power didn't feel so important anymore now that I had real feelings for Simone.

I schooled my expression. "I'll do whatever I can to help you through it."

I at least owed her a try since I'd spent a fortune of her money trying to save my momma.

She sniffed and stared up at me with watery eyes. "Thank you," she said, voice shaky.

I risked giving her a smile. I'm sure it looked more like a grimace.

"Receive the Lord's blessing, Gregory Anton. May the Lord bless you and watch over you," the priest said

I turned away and fought the urge not to snatch my hand from her cold clammy ones.

1 MONTH LATER

"Don't you dare try to make me out to be some sniveling bitch who needs her husband around all the time. You said we'd try to make this marriage work and you've been putting in very little effort."

I sighed and rubbed the heel of my hand against my forehead to alleviate the tension headache pounding right above my right eye.

"Paula..." I tried to keep my tone even when I addressed her, though I felt anything but at ease. "How many times do we have to go through this? Your father's death and you putting me in charge left me with a lot of responsibility. Responsibilities that take me out of town on business."

"That's fine, Seth, but you're using it to avoid me."

By avoiding her she meant avoiding fucking her and I was avoiding fucking her. I'd just arrived home to find her laid out on the bed in her best lingerie, waiting for me. I cringed. Just being in the room with her made my skin crawl. The thought of actually having sex with her turned my stomach. I'd been avoiding it for two months and was running out of excuses.

"I'm not avoiding you," I lied.

I checked the contents of my travel bag, quickly. Fully aware of the fact that Paula was becoming increasingly angry. I knew she would get angrier when she transitioned into talking about her actual grievance with me.

She kept rambling. I zipped my bag and picked it up from the bed we now shared.

"I want a baby, Seth," she screamed

My spine stiffened. I gave her a sidelong glance. "Get a dog,

Paula. We've discussed this. Neither one of us are prepared for children.

What I really wanted to say was there isn't a chance in hell. Why would I bring a child into the world with a woman who acted like a violent toddler? She was off her fucking rocker if she thought she would carry my child.

I backed away a little as she came towards me. Her fists clenched then unclenched. I dug my fingernails into my palm, afraid that I might hit her back if she hit me and knew once I started hitting her, I wouldn't stop until she was bloody.

"If I wanted a fucking dog, I'd buy a dog. I want a baby and you promised me one."

"I told you I'd think about it," I said.

"There's nothing to think about!"

I stared her down. "Get a hold of yourself. I will leave and not come back."

She smirked. "With nothing."

"No, with job offers. I could leave today and be employed with a six-figure salary tomorrow."

As soon as she'd made me head of her father's company, the job offers came flying in. The smirk fell from her face.

She clucked her tongue. "I'm sorry." She gave me her usual response. "Yelling at you was in poor taste." She tried to sound remorseful and failed, sounding fake instead.

"We'll talk about this when I return."

I picked up my bag and made my way downstairs and out of the house. I had no plans of ever returning.

SIMONE 1 MONTH LATER

"Simone."

The sound of my name being called stilled my feet. I knew immediately who the voice belonged to. I pivoted to find Vincent jogging across the parking lot towards me. Damn he was fine. His deep wave, lowcut Caesar seemed to be freshly cut. His big six-foot, two hundred-pound body was still cut to precision, which was to be expected since he was a gym trainer. That was how I had met him. I had been trying to get some extra weight of these thighs if mine during high school, while he worked to get between them.

His Issey Miyake cologne reached me before he did, causing flashes of our past together to stiffen my nipples. I let my mind sink into the memory of our limbs tangled together in white satin sheets, all thousand fibers gently caressing our sweat slicked skin. Then there was that one time, I was riding him in the back of the movie theatre as his finger gripped my hips too tightly. Or my favorite; him with his hand at my throat as he fucked me on the warm hood of his car in the dark parking lot. For two years in undergrad, all we did was fuck and have fun. I didn't love him, and he didn't love me, but I had at least expected respect and honesty from him. Which was why I had tried my best to beat his ass when I found out after a quickie on my sofa that he had a whole girlfriend for six months he hadn't told me about.

"Vincent..." I spoke his name coolly. I cocked an eyebrow and a hip and folded my arms across my chest.

He laughed. "Don't start, Simone."

I chuckled and allowed him to pull me into a hug. There were really no hard feelings. I just didn't like that he lied to me. He had since apologized, and I couldn't stay mad because we really didn't have a title. We were quintessential friends with benefits.

"How are you, Vincent?" I asked.

"I'm fucking awesome. How about you, beautiful?"

I answered him, and we stood there having small talk for a while. "We should get dinner and catch up," he said after a while.

It was on the tip of my tongue to say no. I was still soft in the middle from what had happened with Seth. But then I thought about it, did I want to keep letting my life revolve around that situation?

"Sure, when?" I asked.

"Like right now," he said.

He grabbed my hand and pulled me in the direction of the Ybor strip. There were restaurants lining both sides of the street. Even though Seth was still sending me money, I had just applied at a few. I took a two-month break from working to get my mind right and decided against ever working in anyone else's home again. In Seth's house, I'd seen enough private drama to last me a lifetime.

We stopped at Hamburger Mary's. It was crowded. We had to wait twenty minutes then make our way through a crowd of people. We were on the second floor, overlooking the strip. After ordering, I couldn't help it, I told Vincent everything about Seth and me. He listened without judgment.

"You agreeing to this meal makes sense now. Just last month I called you and you weren't trying to deal with me, but now suddenly you're down?

His eyes dropped to my lips, then he licked his own like he could already taste me.

"What are you trying to do? Get over him by getting under me?" His fingers caressed the underside of my wrist, sending a tingly feeling throughout my body.

I shifted in my seat crossing my legs and squeezing my

thighs together. "That might actually work." I was horny and tired of thinking about Seth, so even if it only got my mind off him temporarily, I welcomed the reprieve.

His reaction was priceless. His eyes widened and he sat up straight in his chair. "Really?" he asked.

I nodded. "Yes," I said, but he seemed momentarily distracted.

He squinted. "Aye Simone, the white boy you were telling me about... Is he pale, blond, about my size, my height?"

I frowned. "How'd you know that?"

He nodded his head toward the door. "The one right behind you don't look very happy. As a matter of fact, he looks like he wants to square up and he's heading this way. Let me find out you fuck Ken doll replicas. Is he even anatomically correct?" He laughed with mischief in his eyes, showing no fear, he casually leaned back in his seat.

I turned around to find Seth heading through the crowded restaurant in our direction with Robert hot on his heels. They were both wearing gym clothes.

I was more surprised to see him and Robert together than actually seeing him. His office was right around the corner. Halfway to our table, Robert reached out and grabbed Seth by the arm, stopping him. He leaned in and whispered something to Seth that caused him to cut his eyes at me. He violently snatched his arm away and continued my way. I couldn't wrap my mind around seeing them together, friendly. Robert was fucking his wife. How the fuck did they go from that to whatever this was?

He came to a halt right in front of me at the table. Robert stopped right behind him, looking around the restaurant nervously.

"This isn't the time," he mumbled under his breath.

It was like he said nothing at all. Seth eyed Vincent, sizing him up.

"What are you doing here, Mr. Alquist?" I asked.

His brows rose. "Can I talk to you? Alone."

"Not right now. I'm here with a friend."

"Does your friend know about me?"

The energy wafting off him was violent and possessive. I could physically feel it, but Vincent wasn't moved by it. But that was his personality. He didn't take shit seriously.

Vincent shoved his hand between us in an attempt to introduce himself. "Hey, I'm the friend."

Neither one of us acknowledged him. Seth wouldn't stop staring at me and I couldn't look away.

"Does he, Simone?" Seth asked, but I couldn't hear him.

Out of my peripheral, I saw a white lady in a gown who caught my attention. With her hair all askew, it looked like she was floating our way, looking like an angry ghost. I swore I was tripping at first. I blinked hard and when she was inches from us, I realized it was Seth's wife. She looked like she had aged a considerable amount on two months. Her already small frame was emancipated and her face gaunt. The next part was sudden and happened in slow motion

"You're a liar," she screamed, lifted her arm and swung.

Seth never even got a chance to face her. The sound of his flesh being sliced was sickening. Seth stumbled forward. I gasped. The metallic taste of blood filled my mouth. I choked, coughed and spit. I did my best not to gag on it.

I watched Seth fall to the ground a pair of gold shear sticking from his side. I wanted to help but I was frozen. I heard the screams, mostly Seth's wife. She was hysterical accusing him of trying to leave her.

Then as if she suddenly realized what she'd done, she stopped. Her eyes fell to Seth, then side to side." No, no, no," she screamed.

Her entire body shook and vibrated from the realization of what she'd done. Then, like a bat out of hell, she took off running. Her bare feet slammed against the concrete sounding like suppressed gun fire. Nobody even attempted to stop her as she made her way downstairs. What felt like only seconds later, there was the sound of the crunching of metal, the tinkling of glass as it shattered.

My heartbeat too fast to be healthy. My head swam. I clamped my hands over my mouth to hold in my scream. I'd just watched my lover being murdered by his wife. I couldn't breathe. My heart hurt. Blood pounded against my ears, it felt like someone was sitting on my chest. Suddenly... everything went black.

***

When I woke up hours later in the hospital, the doctor told me I'd had a panic attack. I found out Seth wasn't dead. His wife had killed herself and injured another man when she tried to drive drunk after stabbing Seth. Next the police came with the questions. A big burly white officer stood at my bed side and drilled me.

Did the Alquist have marital problems?

Did Mrs. Alquist drink a lot?

Had she ever been violent towards her husband or the staff?

Yes. Yes. And yes. I recalled the time she threatened me and the time I suspected her of throwing something at Robert. I guess Robert told them the rest because they asked me about the affair. I told them I had indeed caught them fucking and she'd threatened me. Surprisingly, my situation with Seth was never brought up.

After being released from the hospital I wanted to visit Seth in the ICU, but after what happened, I realized it was officially time to let whatever it was that had developed between him and I go. Too much bad had happened.

***

Days later, I watched on the news as everything unfolded. They skewered Mrs. Alquist, told all her business. They speculated that she'd stabbed Seth because he had left her after an affair with her assistant. He'd been living in a hotel for over a month after reporting her abuse to the police. In return, she'd reported that she'd been receiving death threats and said she suspected Seth of doing it, but she had no proof of any threats.

They'd even interviewed Robert. He said he hadn't heard of any threats or letters or text. I couldn't believe I'd been working for them and didn't know how fucking dysfunctional they were. A few times I picked up the phone to call and check up on Seth, mostly because I wanted to know how he was doing. I was still curious about him and Robert but decided against it. I threw myself headfirst into school and kept the TV and radio off.

4 MONTHS LATER

"You good, Simone?" Vincent asked after he'd brought the last of my boxes into my new condo and set it down while I sat on my newly purchased sofa rubbing my sore feet and regretting not hiring movers.

After the incident with Mrs. Alquist, her father's company had given me a quarter of a million dollars not to speak to reporters about what I'd saw that day. Vincent had made a grip also.

"Yes, thank you. I'm good." He had volunteered to help me move.

Vincent ran both hand over his head. "Well I'm about to get out of here. I have a date."

After the incident with Seth, Vincent and I decided to be just friends. Well, he decided. He joked he couldn't fuck with me because I had crazy white people stabbing each other around me.

"Bye, have fun." I waved him off from my seat on the sofa.

He left locking the door behind him. I looked around my new place and couldn't believe I owned it outright. I'd used my hush money to buy it. I paid off all four years of law school, and I was still receiving money from Seth each month. I wanted to unpack, but it was late. I decided to wait until the next morning. My energy was depleted. For a while I just sat there, listening to the ceiling fan oscillate.

Just as I pushed myself up from the sofa to go shower and crawl my weary ass into bed there was a knock at the door. I figured Vincent had left something behind.

"Coming," I yelled.

I walked to the door and swung it open without even thinking to look and see who it was. My eyes went wide, they had to be as big as saucers. Instead of Vincent it was Seth, dressed in a polo shirt and khakis. He was holding a Jake's Cantina bag. I took a step back.

"I told you you'd be seeing me again. Why do you look so surprised, Simone?" He smiled at me like he hadn't been bleeding to death the last time I saw him.

"What are yo—" I started then got choked up.

I hadn't seen him since that day. He had been so bloody and pale. Pressure built in my chest and I had to get rid of it somehow. I busted out crying. He dropped the bags he was holding to the floor then reached out and pulled me to him. Running his hand through my hair he rocked me as I cried into his polo shirt.

EPILOGUE- SIMONE

The day Seth knocked on my door was the day we started over. We spent months actually getting to know each other and coming to grips with the fact that his wife had tried to kill him. He went to counseling, avoided paparazzi, sold his wife's company, and then opened his own firm.

Months later, he lived up to all the promises he made while he was married. On our wedding day, we stood facing each other, just the two of us in a wedding chapel in Vegas as he recited his vows to me. He looked so handsome in his navy-blue tailored suit. I decided to forego the traditional wedding dress and wore a blood red bandage dress that hugged my curves in all the right place.

"Before you, I felt like I'd already lost my entire world. But then you came along and there was something in those eyes of yours, something that was so beautiful, so safe and warm. I felt at home with you. I feel at home with you and if you allow me, I'll spend the rest of my days making you happy. I love you, Simone."

Teary eyed I mouth the words back and nodded. Moments later, the Elvis impersonator said, "You may kiss the bride."

We left the wedding chapel hand-in- hand, ready to start our new life.

BACK TO THE PRELUDE: SETH

"Why would you want to kill your wife?" The bartender asked.

I raised my shirt and flashed him the fresh bandages that covered the three-inch gash I'd just had stitched up, a result of one of Paula's tantrums. Her father had belittled her in front of his colleagues. I took the brunt end of her rage in the form of a letter opener to the gut.

He visibly cringed. "Why not just leave? That's what we tell women to do."

I told him my predicament.

"So, she drinks a lot and has a temper. You can work with that. You ever seen the movie Gaslight?"

I raised an eyebrow. "No never. What's it about. Give me the CliffsNotes."

He leaned in where I could hear him over the smooth jazz playing over the sound system. "Well this ruthless motherfucker attempts to make his wife think she's crazy so he can throw her in the insane asylum to get some jewels or her money. I don't remember which, because there's tons of movies that followed it. But if it was me, I'd go that route. You said her fathers on his last leg. Until then make her life hell. Make her paranoid. Then when he goes take away everything else that she loves. Make sure the booze is readily available for her to drink and let nature do its job. Accidents happen to drunk people all the time. She falls down the stairs, walks in front of a moving car, combines Ambien and vodka and never wakes up. Make sure you make a police report to document her abuse, just don't press charges.

I listened intently then I thought about it. It was a ridiculous idea, but pain killers and the scotches had my judgment hazy.

"What's your name?" I asked.

"I'm Robert." He held out his hand for me to shake.

I introduced myself. Robert was perfect to help execute his plan. He was Paula's type. Young, Black and handsome. In reality, he was more her type than me. He was what she wanted. But she would never let her father know. That was where I came in. I was the trophy husband her father expected her to have and sometimes I think that was why she got so angry with me.

I knew she was looking for an assistant. I offered Robert a huge pay day, and I made sure he was in the right place at the right time. Then we put the plan into action. He slipped threatening letters into the mailbox, sent some text messages, vandalized her car. Spread rumors about me cheating on her with various women in the office and made sure the liquor cabinets stayed stocked. Then he made sure that him and the letters disappeared when she got the police involved. Then her father died. I made promises and stayed long enough to get her hopes up, then I left. I thought she would commit suicide, not stab me in the fucking back.

I actually felt bad that she almost killed someone because of me, but I made sure him, and his family never had to worry about money again. What I hadn't planned was falling in love with Simone. The night. after seeing her at Allister's, I'd googled her out of curiosity and found her in LinkedIn.

Coincidentally, one of the lawyers she interned for during undergrad happened to be the best criminal defense attorney in Florida and her uncle. She would make the perfect witness to Paula's abuse and if need be, she was close to the one person who could keep me out of prison. Tempting as she was, I hadn't planned on even touching her sexually until the footage, then I couldn't resist. I explained Robert away by simply telling her that I had known him long before he was fucking Paula.

In the end, it all worked out.
I got the girl.
I got the money.
I got my revenge.

Damon is coming...
You have no concept of how truly bad I could
be, Sala. That's why I need you. You're my conscience.
-Damon. Son of Adam and Eve.